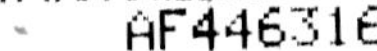

OTHER BOOKS BY MONIQUE MARTIN

OUT OF TIME SERIES

Out of Time: A Time Travel Mystery (Book #1)
When the Walls Fell (Book #2)
Fragments (Book #3)
The Devil's Due (Book #4)
Thursday's Child (Book #5)
Sands of Time (Book #6)
A Rip in Time (Book #7)
A Time of Shadows (Book #8)
Voyage in Time (Book #9)
Revolution in Time (Book #10)
Expedition in Time (Book #11)
Race Through Time (Book #12)
That Time in Paris (Book #13)
Secrets in Time (Book 14)

OUT OF TIME CHRISTMAS NOVELLAS

In Time for Christmas
Christmas in New York
The Christmas Express
Christmas in London
The Christmas Curse

SAVING TIME SERIES

Jacks Are Wild (Book #1)
Aloha, Jack (Book #2)
Nairobi Jack (Book #3)
Maverick Jack (Book #4)

THE BLAZE SERIES

The Blaze (Book #1)
Mirror (Book #2)
Legacy (Book #3)

HOLLYWOOD HEROES SERIES

The Frame (Book #1)
The Curse (Book #2) - coming soon!

The Christmas Curse

MONIQUE MARTIN

Don't miss a new release! Sign up for Monique's newsletter here:
http://moniquemartin.weebly.com

ACKNOWLEDGMENTS

As always this book would not have been possible without the help of many people. I would like to thank Michael, Eddie & Carole, Mom & George, Dad & Anne, Gillian, The Diaspora, Robin, and especially Laura for everything they did to make this book possible.

I'd also like to thank the thousands of people who help preserve the past through books, websites, museums, and sheer will.

CHAPTER ONE

A S THE CAR TURNED down the drive and Grey Hall loomed ahead of them, Simon almost told the driver to turn around. It was an absurd and childish thought. He dismissed it immediately, but the unease he felt whenever he returned here settled into his bones like a winter chill.

Simon had never had any interest in being a baronet or even much in being a Cross. If it hadn't been for his grandfather, he probably would have left England far sooner than he had. As it was, he'd been a good little soldier and gone to public school and then Oxford, as was expected. It wasn't until after university and his parents' deaths that he'd finally found the courage to leave England and Grey Hall behind.

Next to him, Elizabeth and Charlotte peered out of the car window as they drew closer to the great house. They were excited to spend the holidays here. He'd been reluctant at first to bring Charlotte here at all. Memories of a childhood spent at Grey Hall were not pleasant. However, he thought with relief as he not only saw but felt the warmth of his daughter's smile, her memories were not his.

Although it was unusual for Sussex, a light dusting of fresh snow settled over the broad lawn of the large estate, a thin blanket of the season. The tires of the hired car crunched loudly as it glided smoothly across the gravel drive until it stopped in the shadow of his past.

Over the years, they'd spent a few summers and the odd week here. Both Charlotte and Elizabeth enjoyed it immensely, and so he'd agreed when Elizabeth suggested they spend Christmas here this year. His early memories of Christmas at Grey Hall had long since been neatly packed away, nothing worth revisiting. Cold inside and out.

He looked down at Charlotte as her eager eyes scanned the scenery and she shared a contagious laugh of delighted anticipation with Elizabeth. If he had any say in the matter, and he did, Christmas at Grey Hall would meet all of his daughter's expectations. He promised himself that she would only have fond memories.

The car came to a stop before the oversized front entry doors. Not waiting for the driver, Simon opened his door and then helped Charlotte and Elizabeth out. Despite the long flight and subsequent drive, Charlotte bounced on the balls of her feet in anticipation, the tiny pebbles of the drive crunching beneath her feet. She gazed up at the imposing edifice of Grey Hall with nothing but delight shining in her eyes. She was nothing like he had been at her age—sullen and lonely. If he had done nothing else with his life, at least he had made sure of that.

Elizabeth arched her back, working out the kinks of intercontinental travel, and smiled up at him as she took his hand. There was a kindness in her eyes, a softness that soothed his anxiety. They hadn't discussed it really, but there hadn't been a need to. She understood. More than anyone ever had, she understood what coming here meant to him.

Charlotte bounded ahead of them, but before she reached the entrance, the front doors opened. Mr. and Mrs. Carter, the caretakers of Grey Hall, beamed at them. A little more anxiety eased inside Simon at the sight of the couple.

"Welcome home, Sir Simon."

"Good to see you, John," Simon said, shaking the older man's hand. "You're looking well, Hannah."

After his Aunt Virginia had passed away, Simon had replaced most of the staff, including the butler and housekeeper, and hired the Carters to oversee Grey Hall in his absence. They were a genial couple in their mid-sixties who had happily spent their life in service.

"We're glad to have you home, sir," Hannah said. There was a warm light in her eyes that made crossing the threshold a bit less of a trial for him. "And you, Lady Cross, and of course young Miss Charlotte."

Charlotte gave them a little wave as she hurried inside.

Simon knew Elizabeth was still uncomfortable with the use of her title but relented, knowing that while the custom wasn't important to her it was to others.

She greeted the couple warmly then stepped past them into the foyer. She paused, and Simon watched the lights of the decorations reflect in her eyes as she took it all in. "It looks beautiful."

The great hall was tastefully decorated for the season with two large and elegant Christmas trees standing sentinel on either side of the room. Garlands of green boughs with large red ribbons draped from the railing of the minstrels' gallery above, while the light from several candelabras glowed between a dozen or so deep red poinsettias.

Hannah tugged on her fingers nervously. "I hope we haven't overstepped. Sir Simon did express a desire for the great hall to be ... appropriately adorned for the season."

Elizabeth reached forward and squeezed her hand. "It's lovely."

And it was. Too much so perhaps. The lights were perfectly spaced on the tree, the ornaments—all silver and gold and glass—hung with military precision, and there was not a stray strand of tinsel or a dead needle to be seen. It was a store window, not a home. His parents would have loved it.

"You did a wonderful job," Elizabeth went on as she walked further in to admire their work. "It should be in a magazine."

The Carters blushed at the compliment.

"It's so pretty!" Charlotte exclaimed, turning in delight as she took it all in before suddenly stopping and turning to her parents. "Can we still have a Charlie Brown tree?"

Elizabeth walked over and put an arm around her shoulders. "Wouldn't be Christmas without one. We get to do our damage in the drawing room," she said with an inquiring glance at the Carters, who nodded. "Dancing Santa and all."

Simon sighed for effect, mostly, as he came to their side. "I had hoped that we could do without *that* particular tradition this year."

Elizabeth laughed, looping her arm through his. "That depends. Have you been a good boy?" she asked softly.

He cleared his throat. "Elizabeth."

She laughed again and then turned back to the Carters. "Thank you for this. It really is lovely. If we have anyone over, we won't let them leave this room."

The Carters exchanged worried looks.

"We won't be having anyone over," Simon assured them. Planning for parties, even small ones, at estates like Grey Hall was not a spur-of-the-moment endeavor, especially with the skeleton staff he'd kept on.

Regardless, there was no one to invite. With Aunt Virginia gone, he had no family left. There were a few dozy cousins that he'd rather avoid, but other than that, the only family he had was standing in this room, and they were more than enough.

"I'm going to explore, okay?" Charlotte called from the top of the stairs and then disappeared without waiting for an answer.

"Just . . . be careful," Simon said to the empty spot where his daughter had been. She knew his usual admonitions well enough that he wasn't too worried.

As they walked up the stairs, Simon tried to ignore the chill that ran through him. The ghosts of his past remained here—silent and invisible, but here nonetheless. He was glad he was considering selling it. Now, he just had to find the courage to tell his wife.

"All right?" she said, leaning in close and speaking softly.

He smiled in reassurance, clasping his hand over hers. A lie of omission, perhaps, but allowable.

"Still glad we came?" she asked a little unsurely.

"I am," he said and meant it sincerely. It could be, after all, his last Christmas at Grey Hall.

CHARLOTTE THREW OPEN THE doors to her bedroom. It was three times as big as her bedroom back home and looked like something out of a storybook—bright and airy with high coffered ceilings and an excess of windows. She even had her own little sitting room area and an enormous four-poster bed.

Paddington Bear sat in the middle of it, waiting for her. She picked him up, gently plucking at his ears. She was too old for stuffed animals now—she was nearly twelve!—but he still had a place in her heart. She set him down in the rocking chair by her old toys and walked over to the windows. The drapes had already been pulled, and the late afternoon sun shone through them.

Her room overlooked one of the gardens, not that there was much to see right now. Bits of green and brown poked out through the light covering of white snow. It looked so still, so peaceful. She wished her father could see it the way she did. She was just about to turn away from it when an owl swooped down to land on the top edge of a barren arbor. She wasn't sure if she'd imagined it or not at first. Its body was white, with light brown and pale grey feathers on its back.

When its flat, white, disc-shaped face swiveled and looked right up at her, she gasped.

"Don't move," she whispered to it and took off like a shot out of her room and down the stairs.

By the time she grabbed her coat—one of her parents' many "rules for exploring"—and went outside, it was gone. Hopeful she'd catch sight of it again, Charlotte turned in a slow circle, but the owl was nowhere to be seen. If her book on birds of prey was to be believed, she didn't think it had traveled too far. She squinted at the small copse of trees nearby, looking for a nest in the hollows of the trees, but that didn't seem likely. These were skinny silver birch. Owls needed something a bit more substantial. There were other trees, but somehow, she knew that it lived in the Dark Woods. It was full of beech and oak and even a few pine. But that was another of her parents' rules: Don't go into the Dark Woods alone.

She'd gone there with her father a few times on a walk or riding. Despite the folklore about them, he'd assured her that they weren't haunted, that no evil witch lived there. She'd heard stories of the Witch of the Woods from servants at the Hall since she could remember. In the end, she decided it was just another

Boogey Man meant to keep kids away from places they weren't supposed to go. Her father told her that the woods were dangerous because they housed the now-hidden remnants of an old well.

Still, it was tempting.

But if she was going to break rules, it was better not to do it on the first day of their stay, she thought with a sigh. Befriending an owl would be amazing, but as Mom would say, today, it just wasn't in the cards. Maybe she was better off exploring the ruins. At least that's what she called them. They were really just the shell of the old house that had originally been built here before they put up Grey Hall. There wasn't much to it now—just a few crumbling walls and an old stone fireplace and part of the chimney—but she liked to imagine it was where some great Elizabethan knight had fought and died tragically for his lady love, or even better, vice versa. Women could die tragically too.

Another epic story of good triumphing over evil already starting to form in her imagination, she started to wander toward it when she had the unmistakable sensation of being watched. Turning back toward the house, she half expected to see her mother or father calling her back inside, but there was no one there. Maybe the owl had returned. She scanned the roofline with hope in her heart. Nothing. She looked lower and then stopped when she saw a figure in her bedroom window looking out at her from behind the curtain. It wasn't her mom or dad and didn't look like either of the Carters. She was too far away to see who it was clearly. She waved, but the figure abruptly disappeared.

"Okaaay," she said with a sigh. People were weird.

With a shrug, she set off for the ruins. They weren't far, and she would have just enough time to tell herself her "new and improved" version of Saint George and the Dragon—where the princess and the dragon lived happily ever after—before she'd have to go back inside.

As she walked, though, she felt that same sensation again—of being watched. She turned back, but there was no one there. A shiver ran down her spine, and she pulled her coat more tightly around her. It was probably just her imagination getting revved up. With one last glance at the manor house, she trudged across the field to the old, forgotten ruins.

CHAPTER TWO

CHARLOTTE COULDN'T SLEEP AND rolled over again with a sigh, trying to find a comfortable position that would allow her mind to slow down enough to fall asleep. But all she could think about was what she would do tomorrow: the places she'd explore, the decorations they'd put up for Christmas. Christmas! Just the thought of it was enough to keep her awake. She loved Christmas, which felt a little silly to say; everyone loved Christmas. Well, not everyone. But not many seemed to love it like she did. Christmas was *her* special holiday.

Memories of traveling back in time to New York to help Charlie Blue, meeting Mark Twain, and even seeing a real angel, flooded her mind. Christmas always brought something special. She could hardly wait to see what this year had in store, not that they were traveling back in time or were likely to meet anyone that exciting this year. Grey Hall was gift enough, although not for everyone she knew. She didn't know exactly why, but this wasn't her father's favorite place. Her mom had said something about bad memories, but neither of them really told her much more.

Since the first time she'd come here, she'd tried to imagine her father as a boy living in the Hall, but it was impossible. He was . . . Dad. She knew he had been a boy here; she'd even seen the portrait of him in short pants that he threatened to burn each time they visited, but the image of him as he was now— big and strong and sure—was impossible to replace with something else.

The grandfather clock down the hall chimed softly. Midnight. With another sigh, she rolled over again and closed her eyes, counting the soft chimes. *Nine, ten, eleven, twelve.*

Sigh.

It was no use. She wasn't going to be able to sleep. There were no televisions except for the little old set in the kitchen. She did have her tablet, though the Wi-Fi was spotty in her room; her parents had probably done that on purpose. Time to go old-school.

Pulling aside the covers, Charlotte slipped on her robe over her snowman pajamas and found her slippers. She browsed the few books she'd left in her room, but they were all for babies. She was nearly grown up now. It was a good thing there was a massive library downstairs, she thought and headed for the door.

The hallway was chilly, and she tightened the sash on her robe as she padded quietly down the hall to the stairs as dimly lit wall sconces with flickering bulbs simulating candles lit her way.

Having to lean back to get it moving, she pulled open the heavy door to the library and turned on the lights before closing the door behind her. Her parents wouldn't be thrilled to find her still up. But what they didn't know . . .

Now, *these* were books, she thought as she gazed up at high shelf after high shelf filled with book after book. The library was bigger than their living room and dining room back home put together—and those were pretty big. The room was all dark wood and smelled like leather and old books. She loved that smell. She would totally buy a candle with that scent and made a note to email the suggestion to Yankee Candle tomorrow.

Having spent plenty of time here before, Charlotte knew exactly what section she wanted to go to. She dragged the library ladder to the right spot and climbed up the spiral steps to peruse the section of Christmas books. A dozen or so old hardbound books with fading gilt lettering stared back. *Holly and Mistletoe, Riverdale Stories, Robin's Christmas Eve . . . A Christmas Carol.* She grinned—perfect—and took it off the shelf.

She'd only been a baby when her parents had gone back in time to help Charles Dickens write it, but she'd made them tell her the story at least a dozen times. Tucking the fading gold book under her arm carefully, she climbed back down.

She glanced guiltily toward the door; her parents wouldn't be pleased to find her out of bed in the middle of the night. She *could* go upstairs to read, but stories always seemed better when she read them in the library. She'd just start it here and go up in a bit. She settled herself into one of the enormous leather wingback reading chairs, smoothing out a soft chenille throw over her legs as she curled up to read.

She knew the story well enough to write it, but there was something about seeing the words on the page, losing herself between the covers. And this book was different—although they weren't in the story, her parents were part of it.

She snuggled down and opened the book, running her fingers over the colorful swirling pattern of the endpapers before turning the page.

Marley was dead, to begin with. There is no doubt whatever about that. The register of his burial . . .

Her nose itched.

Charlotte rubbed the back of her hand across it, only vaguely awake before snuggling deeper into her blanket, but that movement brought her to just enough of a conscious state to realize something else. She wasn't in her bed and . . . someone was staring at her. She knew it down to her bones.

Busted.

Expecting to see her mother or father with disapproving looks on their faces, she was startled nearly out of her skin when she opened her eyes and saw a stranger leaning down close and staring right at her.

Instinct took over, and she screamed. She hadn't finished hers before his eyes went wide with shock, and he screamed right along with her.

Somehow, she gathered herself before he did. His surprisingly high-pitched shriek continued as she stared silently at him, waiting for him to finish.

His face was round, slightly reddened at the cheeks, with light brown hair poking up from his head as if he'd just woken up. He was kind of sweet-looking, actually.

Charlotte stared at him as he continued to scream until he finally ran out of breath. He panted once and then stood up straight, still looking shocked.

He was a little on the roly-poly side, the buttons of his waistcoat straining against his belly. He wore high-waisted breeches, a long cutaway coat with tails, and a too-frilly cravat. He looked a little like he'd just walked off the set of *Jane Eyre*—or had been taking a nap on the set of *Jane Eyre*—and continued to stare at her in astonished bewilderment.

She wasn't exactly frightened of him, but her parents had taught her to be cautious of strangers, especially those that showed up out of the blue in the middle of the night *inside her house.*

"Who are you?" she demanded, getting out of her chair to put some distance between them.

He clamped a hand over his mouth as he drew a gasping breath, pointing his other hand at her as he took a step back. "Y-you can see me."

It wasn't a question. It was a statement. A horrified statement.

"Of course I can," she replied confused. "Who are you? What are you doing here? My parents are—"

"Oh, no-no-no-no," he said, shaking his head and holding up both hands to stave off something. "Y-you're far too young. This is not right. Oh dear, oh dear, oh dear."

He looked on the verge of panic, but despite her shock at his being there—where he definitely should not be—Charlotte didn't feel threatened by him. If anything, he looked like he was the one who was frightened.

"Too young?" She took a step forward about to inform him that she was only a little more than a year away from being a teenager, but he held up his hands again.

"No. No. No," he said again shaking his head. "This cannot be. This must not be. The others will—"

"Charlotte!"

That was her father's voice—loud, worried, and just down the hall.

Panic struck the intruder's cherubic face again before he turned back to her. "I don't suppose we can pretend this never happened, can we?"

"Charlotte!" her father called out, closer than before.

Before she could reply to either her father or the other man, he glanced at the door one last time and then scurried toward the bookcase. He paused there, shaking his head fretfully again, and muttered "Oh dear" once more before walking straight through the wall.

Straight. Through. The. Wall.

Holy macaroni!

The door to the library opened with a jerk, and her father and mother spilled inside.

"Are you all right?" Simon asked anxiously. "Charlotte?"

Her mom came to her side and took hold of her arms gently. "Sweetie, what happened?"

Charlotte gaped at the bookcase, the solid bookcase, that the man had just passed through. "I saw . . ."

"What did you see?" her father demanded, fear and concern giving his voice a hard edge. "What happened? Why did you scream?"

"I . . . I saw a ghost."

Her mother and father exchanged glances before her dad knelt in front of her. "A ghost? What do you mean?"

Charlotte opened her mouth to answer, but her mother spoke first.

"Simon," she said, sounding much calmer. They both turned to her as she held up the discarded book and gave it a little shake.

He read the title quickly and sighed. "*A Christmas Carol.*" He pushed out another breath and looked at her reproachfully. "Charlotte."

"It wasn't that!" she insisted, annoyed they'd dismissed her claim so easily. She'd seen a real ghost! Or had she? It all seemed like a dream now.

"What have I told you about reading things like this so late?"

"But it wasn't a dream, I don't think," she added, ruining her argument.

Her parents shared another look, this one all-too-familiar—a frustrated but fond sort of "what are we going to do with her?"

Charlotte pursed her lips in annoyance.

"Come back to bed," Elizabeth said finally.

"And no more late-night reading," Simon said, taking the book and putting it down on the end table. "And certainly not down here. We've discussed this, Charlotte."

She was ready to argue with them, but her parents had The Look on their faces, and all she could do was sigh. What could she say? It had certainly felt real, but they had a point; she had fallen asleep

reading about ghosts. As her father had taught her—
the simplest explanation was usually the right one.

"I know. I'm sorry."

As they left the library, Charlotte glanced one
last time at the bookcase before she let her parents
lead her back to her room.

THE FOLLOWING MORNING, SIMON poured himself
another cup of coffee. He had trouble going back
to sleep after Charlotte's little midnight escapade.
Between her and Elizabeth's proclivity for finding
trouble, it was a miracle he ever slept at all.

Silently, he offered to top off Elizabeth's cup, but
she shook her head. "I've had enough to wake the
dead."

A few minutes later Charlotte came stumbling
in, a little bleary-eyed and distracted.

"Well rested, I see," Simon remarked.

Charlotte muttered something and shuffled to
the side table with the serving trays on it. She lifted
one of the silver lids, and he heard her whisper rever-
ently, "Bacon."

"Just a few," Simon told her as he sipped his coffee
and returned his attention to the newspaper.

Charlotte added some eggs and a piece of toast
to her plate before taking her seat at the dining table.
She drank down half of her glass of orange juice in
one go before digging in.

Over the edge of his paper, Simon observed her carefully. Other than looking tired—no surprise given her antics last night nor her usual slow start in the morning—she looked no worse for the wear.

He put aside the paper. "Your mother and I are going into town this morning to do a little shopping. Would you like to come too or stay here? It will take an hour or two, I'd guess."

She slathered far too much marmalade on her toast. "Is it okay if I stay here?"

"You don't want to come?" Elizabeth asked, unable to keep the disappointment from her voice.

"I barely got to explore at all yesterday. Can we go tomorrow? Maybe get a little tree?"

"We can do that," Elizabeth said, sounding assuaged.

"And Mrs. Carter said we could bake cookies later!"

"In that case," Elizabeth said, "I might stay too."

Charlotte grinned and took a bite of her toast, chomping happily.

"Oh, no," Simon said. "This outing was your idea."

Elizabeth made a face, but he knew it was all for show.

"I'm sorry to interrupt, Sir Simon," Mr. Carter said as he came into the dining room, "but there's a call for you. A Mister Wilkes?"

"Ah," Simon said before wiping his mouth with his napkin and standing. "I'll take it in the study."

Mr. Carter gave a small bow and left.

"Who's Mister Wilkes?" Elizabeth asked.

Simon hesitated. "Oh, just some business about the estate. I won't be long."

He hated misleading her, but he wasn't ready to discuss the subject yet. His own thoughts about it were . . . complicated, and he wanted to have some clarity before he told her what he was considering.

Ciarán Wilkes was a real estate developer with whom his attorney had put him in touch when he'd broached the idea of selling Grey Hall. He hadn't expected to hear from the man until after the holidays. There was no rush, after all, and it was just a possibility. He wouldn't do anything without Elizabeth's agreement.

"So," his wife said to Charlotte as he left, "what kind of cookies are we talkin' here?"

CHARLOTTE STOOD AT THE front door waving goodbye to her parents as her father drove away in one of the cars they kept at the Hall. She waited for a beat of two before she ran back inside, heading straight for the library.

She'd stayed up half the night thinking about what had happened. It wasn't a dream. She was sure of it. That man—ghost—had been there. And if he was there once, he might be there again.

Carefully, she closed the door to the library behind her and walked cautiously into the room. "Hello?"

No one answered. A small part of her was afraid, but most of her vibrated with excitement. She'd seen lots of odd and amazing things in her short life; when she thought about it, a conversation with a ghost didn't seem all that strange.

She made her way over to the bookcase that he'd disappeared into and stood before it contemplating what she should do next. Slowly, she lifted her hand and touched it, half-expecting her hand to go right through it. It didn't, and she stifled her sigh of disappointment. That would have been cool.

Not one to give up easily, especially when there was a need for vindication, she felt around the edges of the shelves, looking for some hidden hinge or trap door or something. Teddy Fiske had trick doors in his library; maybe Grey Hall did too.

But no matter what she pulled off the shelf or touched, nothing happened. The bookcase remained a bookcase. Solid and unmovable.

Charlotte wasn't her parents' child for nothing though. She wasn't about to give up so easily.

She took a step back, putting her hands on her hips. "I know you're in there, Mr. . . . whoever you are. I know you're in there."

Nothing.

"Please come out?" she asked again. She gazed at the bookshelf hopefully. "I won't hurt you."

She waited again, but no one appeared. Maybe he was in the next room over, she thought and turned toward the door.

As she did, she nearly crashed into him. He'd appeared behind her, and they both gasped in surprise again.

"You need to stop doing that!" she scolded him.

"I'm sorry. It . . . it's just been so long." He looked at her with those clear blue eyes, pleading for something she didn't understand.

"Who are you?" she asked again. He was wearing those same odd old clothes.

He hesitated, looking around nervously, but he didn't say anything.

She tried again.

"I'm Charlotte Cross," she said, extending her hand out to shake his.

He looked at her hand dejectedly. "I would, but . . ." He moved his hand toward and then *through* hers.

"You *are* a ghost!" she exclaimed.

He didn't seem nearly as thrilled as she was. "Sadly, yes."

Then he seemed to gather himself somewhat, drawing himself up straight, his belly testing the strength of his waistcoat buttons. "I am Ambrose

Cross, and it is my distinct pleasure to meet you, Charlotte." He offered her a somewhat awkward but courtly bow.

She smiled in return and then stopped short. "Cross? Are we related?"

"I am your great, great . . ." He paused, his brow wrinkling in thought as he worked it out, "great, great, great grandfather. Or I was when I was alive."

"What happened to you?" she asked. He wasn't old, or at least he didn't look old. If he'd still been alive, she would guess he was probably in his early to mid-forties.

He looked momentarily surprised then considered her question. "Oh my, that is a story. And—"

Suddenly, two other men walked out of the same bookcase Ambrose had walked through earlier. One was older, maybe sixty with dark hair and a goatee. His clothing was even older looking than Ambrose's. His frock coat was a deep green, and his shirt had frilly cuffs and an even frillier ruffled neckcloth. He stopped abruptly, halfway into the room, glaring in alarm at her and Ambrose.

His companion was younger, mid-thirties, handsome with blond streaks in his floppy brown hair. He looked a little like Leonardo DiCaprio in *Gatsby*, she thought. His clothing was more modern than the others but still not current day. He grinned broadly and a little mischievously, apparently as pleased to see them as his companion was disturbed.

Charlotte looked from the new arrivals back to Ambrose and then back again, unable to fight her smile.

Three ghosts.

This.

Was.

Awesome.

The older man's piercing eyes flashed and then landed on her so forcefully she could feel the weight of them down to her bones before he shifted his intensity back to Ambrose.

"Ambrose!" he bellowed with asperity. "You clay-brained bull calf! What have you done?!"

CHAPTER THREE

T HE OLDER GHOST GLOWERED AT AMBROSE with such ferocity, Charlotte was momentarily afraid for him.

"I am sorry, Phineas," Ambrose said, rushing over to the two other men. "You must believe that I did not mean for this to happen."

Phineas, the older ghost, glared at Ambrose before turning his fury toward Charlotte. "A child," he said bitterly. "And a girl," he added contemptuously.

Charlotte straightened. "That's not very nice."

His eyes flashed at her with indignation, but she was not about to be cowed by him. He huffed out a breath before turning his ire back to Ambrose, who stood before him wringing his hands.

"Explain yourself, fool," he demanded.

"It was an accident. I was simply watching her, and I . . . suppose I manifested." Phineas opened his mouth to no doubt berate him again, but Ambrose plunged on. "I did not mean to. You must believe me. I just lost track of things," he finished timidly.

"Lost track of your corporeal self?" Phineas countered. "I knew you were a blunderbuss, but of all the addlepated, careless, idiotic things to have done, you somehow manage to do the very worst!"

"He said he was sorry," Charlotte put in. She didn't like bullies, ghosts or not.

"Stay out of this, girl!" Phineas bellowed.

She was startled by his reaction and started to respond when the third ghost, the youngest and by far the most handsome of the trio, walked over to her as if he were out for an evening stroll. "Ignore them," he said. "They'll be at it for hours."

He paused, looking her up and down. "I am Sir Nicholas, but my friends call me Nicky."

"Your friends are all dead," Phineas declared before turning his attention back to Ambrose.

Nicky shrugged, unperturbed. "At least I had friends," he replied softly, giving Charlotte a little conspiratorial wink.

"Now, see here," Phineas began, his pique shifting to Nicky.

"Please don't fight," Ambrose said as he hurried after a stalking Phineas. "I am sorry, but . . . well, what's done is done, is it not?"

Phineas sighed heavily and looked to the ceiling—a gesture so like her father Charlotte nearly gasped.

"Yes. There is nothing to be done for it now. We've only wasted another hundred years is all."

"A hundred years?" Charlotte asked.

"We can only manifest into our … physical forms," Ambrose explained, "every one hundred years."

"And we can only be acknowledged by one individual," Phineas continued for him, his anger still not completely abated. "And that, it appears," he added with a beleaguered sigh, "is you."

He said the last word with not quite disgust but something close to it.

She would have been offended, but her thoughts finally caught up with her surprise. "Why is that such a bad thing?" she asked, starting to worry.

Phineas looked like he was about to say something and then his demeanor shifted again, abruptly taking shelter in his anger again. "Because you are a child. What can you possibly do to help us?"

Clearly, she was missing pieces of this conversation. "Help you? How? What's wrong?"

"Other than being ghosts?" Phineas bit out.

"Don't worry about him," Nicky assured her kindly. "He's just prickly."

Phineas snorted.

Ambrose turned to her, smiling sadly. "Unfortunately, we are trapped here. I have been a prisoner of this house for coming on two hundred years. Nicholas for one and," his eyes fell sympathetically on Phineas, "Phineas for three."

"Three hundred years?" Charlotte asked, incredulous.

"Yes," Phineas replied dolefully, his anger seeming to have finally burned itself out, "and now it will be an additional one hundred years before we get another chance." He turned to Ambrose. "I would kill you if you weren't already dead."

"Maybe I can help," Charlotte said quickly. "Solve your problem," she clarified. "Not re-kill Ambrose."

Ambrose looked at her with doe eyes, innocent and filled with hope, but Phineas only snorted again.

"Don't write her off out of hand, old man," Nicky said. "I think you might be underestimating her. She is a Cross after all."

Phineas hummed in displeasure, but at least it was a step up from his anger, Charlotte thought.

"You're all Crosses?" she asked, although her heart already knew that it was true.

"I am Sir Nicholas," Nicky said with a courtly bow. "You've already met Sir Ambrose." Ambrose bowed with a flourish. "And this disagreeable fellow is Sir Phineas. We are your ancestors."

Her face split into a broad grin. "Awesome."

Phineas made another displeased sound, but she ignored him.

"Why are you stuck here? I mean, why you? Are there others?" she asked, realizing there might be more, dozens even. She glanced around, half expecting them to pour out of the bookcases as well.

"We are the lucky few," Nicky said. "It is just the three of us."

"Until Christmas Day," Phineas added darkly.

A chill surged through Charlotte, giving rise to goosebumps that traveled up and down her arms. "What do you mean?"

Abruptly, the door to the library opened. Mrs. Carter and a young housemaid stepped inside. "You must keep better track of things," Mrs. Carter was saying. "Remember, Rachel, you are not meant to be seen or—" She stopped suddenly, and Charlotte worried she might have a heart attack at the sight of the three ghosts.

"Oh, forgive me. I am sorry for interrupting, Miss Charlotte," she said placidly. "I didn't realize you were here."

Or maybe she wouldn't care?

"That's all right," Charlotte replied carefully, glancing between the housekeeper and the ghosts.

If Mrs. Carter saw them, she gave no indication of it. Neither did Rachel.

"We will come back later. If I might," Mrs. Carter asked, gesturing across the room to where a caddy with cleaning supplies sat. "We'll just retrieve those and be out of your way."

"All right," Charlotte said uneasily as Mrs. Carter crossed the room, walking right through Ambrose, who shuddered in response. She would have passed through Sir Phineas too if he hadn't stepped out of her way, glaring bloody murder at her as she passed by.

Mrs. Carter retrieved the caddy, passing through Ambrose again, who giggled this time.

"Tickles," he said wriggling his shoulders.

Mrs. Carter gave him no notice. She couldn't see or hear them.

The housekeeper rejoined Rachel by the library door. "Those cookies will be ready and waiting for you," she said kindly.

"Wonderful," Charlotte managed, although her mind was filled with other things.

With one last smile, Mrs. Carter and Rachel left, closing the door behind them.

"Intolerable," Phineas grumbled.

"She couldn't see you," Charlotte announced "or hear you."

"How clever of you to notice," Phineas said sarcastically.

Charlotte pursed her lips and put her fists to her hips. "Forgive me, but I've only known about ghosts for a few minutes and not three hundred years."

Ambrose gave a short laugh that he tried desperately to squelch, while Nicky laughed in outright delight. "Oh, I *do* like you."

"So I'm the only one who can see and hear you? Not my parents? Or the Carters? Just me?"

"You are the lucky one," Nicky said.

"But why?" Charlotte asked. "Why can't anyone else see you?"

"It's because of the—" Ambrose began but was silenced by Phineas's raised hand.

"It is of no matter," Phineas said, sounding suddenly tired. "It is as it is. As are we."

She could tell he meant something significant by that, but she had no idea what.

"I don't think you should give up so easily, Phineas," Nicky said. "She is a child, but—"

"There is no point in it," Phineas said before taking a deep, steadying breath. "I am sure you mean well, girl, but there is nothing you can do for us. And sadly," he added, "nothing we can do for you."

His anger was gone now, replaced only with sorrow, and it sent another set of chills down Charlotte's spine.

Before she could ask for an explanation, they began to fade. Ambrose looked at her with heartbreak, Nicky with pity, while Phineas's expression was unreadable. She had a bad feeling about all of this. Quite suddenly, this was turning out to be less Scooby-Doo mystery and more *Haunting of Hill House.*

"Wait," she begged, but they dissolved into nothing, leaving her alone in the library again.

"Closed."

That was the second store in town that was closed. Elizabeth would have thought, given the holiday, they all would be doing a brisk business, but Greyswood was anything but brisk. Sadly, she'd seen something similar play out in town after town across Texas when she was growing up—Greyswood was dying. There were half a dozen shuttered businesses and nearly that many with real estate signs out front.

She supposed nothing was immune from hard times, but somehow Greyswood had always seemed immutable, a village stuck in time that would remain—mostly—as it had always been. She should have known better. Recessions hit everywhere, and more often than not, small towns like this were hit the hardest. It wasn't exactly the festive shopping trip she'd had planned.

"Oh, there's a new one!" Elizabeth cried, spotting a new storefront on Alder Road.

Simon pulled their car over to park.

She was glad to see something open. The little pharmacy and market were still going, but so much of the town was shuttered. It made her hopeful to see something new.

"The Prince and the Pauper," she said, reading the sign over the store.

"Hmm," Simon replied distantly.

He'd been distracted all morning, although that wasn't exactly new when it came to shopping together. She was a browse and wander kind of girl, usually happy to spend an afternoon with nothing to show for it other than sore feet and regret over that second soft pretzel. Simon, however, was the seek-and-destroy type. He knew what he wanted, where it was, and how much it should cost before he even crossed the threshold. He was a purposeful hunter; she was a distracted gatherer.

Just as they were about to go inside, his cell phone rang. He glanced at the caller ID and told her that he'd be along in a moment.

The Prince and the Pauper was the kind of store Elizabeth loved—one of those charming boutiques with a little of everything and no two items the same. It sold everything from clothing to earthenware and candles, to handmade Christmas and Yule decorations.

"Ohhh!" Elizabeth cried, closing in on a display of hand-carved ornaments—rings of wood with adorable little painted lovebirds resting on a fresh branch of pine.

"Hello," the storekeeper greeted her. She nodded toward the display. "Those are all done by local artists."

She was an attractive woman in her mid-thirties with a striking streak of premature grey in her otherwise dark brown hair.

"They're great!" Elizabeth told her, admiring a gorgeous porcelain stag ornament and a nearby candle that smelled of cinnamon and citrus. "It all is."

"I try to have a little bit of everything."

"You're the owner?"

The woman nodded. "I am. Fiona Prince."

Elizabeth smiled and gestured toward where the sign hung outside. "Ah, the name of the store."

Fiona gave a short laugh. "I thought it was so clever, but I'm definitely more of a pauper these days."

Elizabeth hated hearing that, especially from a woman who'd obviously put her heart and soul into creating such a unique store.

"Tough going?" she asked, realizing she was the only patron at the moment.

Fiona sighed and nodded. "Looks like I picked the wrong time to return to Greyswood and open up a shop."

Judging from the "For Sale" signs they'd seen in town, she wasn't alone.

"I didn't realize things had gotten so bad here. What happened?"

The woman smiled wanly. "Life, I suppose. Passing us by."

Elizabeth's heart went out to her. Owning a shop was a risky business at the best of times; doing it now . . .

"I'm Elizabeth, by the way," she introduced herself. "Did you grow up here?"

Fiona rearranged a few necklaces on their branch stand. "My family's been here forever. I don't know how many generations, but times change, I suppose. I came back two years ago and blithely opened up shop. Oops."

Elizabeth laughed with her. "Maybe it will pick up next year."

"I'm not sure there's a next year to be had," Fiona admitted.

"Well, I'm here to do my part to make sure there is," Elizabeth said, knowing Simon wouldn't mind the smoke coming off their credit card when she was done.

After that, they were forced to go to the next town over and then the next to find some of the things they needed. On their way back, they stopped at the Thistle & Goose, the most popular pub in Greyswood.

"A pint and a Coke, please," Simon said as he leaned against the bar. "Are you sure you wouldn't rather have a scrumpy?" he asked her with a gleam in his eye.

"Funny," she said. When she'd first come to England with Simon over ten years ago, she'd innocently drunk the harsh cider and paid the price. She was pretty sure she couldn't even smell the stuff now without . . . She shuddered.

An old man stepped toward them. "Sir Simon? Is that you?"

He was small with a fringe of white hair and a bushy mustache to match. He was shadowed by a taller man with dark grey hair, a prominent nose, and eyebrows that had taken on a life of their own. Just like Statler and Waldorf, she thought with a smile.

"Mr. Kingsley," Simon said, greeting them. "Mr. Booth. Good to see you. I'm not sure you ever met my wife Elizabeth."

Both men gave her a little bow. "Lady Cross."

"Elizabeth, please."

They smiled, looking a bit uncomfortable.

"Mr. Kingsley and Mr. Booth are on the village council," Simon said. "Depending on whom you ask, they *are* the village council."

Mr. Kingsley snorted. "Now, now."

"Oh, if the shoe fits. We are bossy-bottoms, aren't we?"

"Not in front of Lady Cross," Mr. Kingsley scolded. "Er, Elizabeth."

"Either is fine," she said, and they looked relieved to be off that particular hook.

It was one of the things that still surprised her about England. She thought the people would be happy to dispense with titles and meet on more equal footing, but almost to a person, here at least, the opposite was true. She supposed there was comfort in tradition.

"I hadn't realized things had gotten so . . . difficult in town," Simon said diplomatically.

"Oh, well. This too shall pass," Kingsley said, though it was clear from his expression that Mr. Booth did not share his friend's optimism. "Tell us, how have you been? Did you bring that darling child of yours with you?"

"We did. She's back at the Hall exploring," Elizabeth said.

"Ah. To spend the day searching for the wonders of the world with the mind and spirit of a child," Kingsley said with a faraway smile.

"You're halfway there," Booth quipped before turning to Simon and Elizabeth. "I'll leave it to you to decide which half."

"Now, now," Kingsley blustered genially at the remark before turning back to the Crosses. "I do hope your daughter has an enjoyable Christmas."

Elizabeth smiled. "She always does."

THIS IS THE WORST *Christmas ever*, Charlotte lamented silently.

"Are you sure you're all right?" her mother asked her. "You never did tell us what you did today."

Charlotte sighed, rolling her green beans across the plate. She *had* told them. More than once actually. She'd told them all about the ghosts the minute they came back from town. They'd listened wide-eyed and then promptly forgotten seconds later. It was strange and very disconcerting. She'd tried to tell them for nearly twenty minutes, but as soon as she finished, they forgot everything that they'd been talking about. They didn't even notice that they were forgetting, either. It was like the conversations never happened.

"I told you, I met three ghosts," she said, mashing a piece of roasted potato with her fork.

"I think I'd remember that," Simon remarked.

"I wish you would," Charlotte said softly.

Her parents exchanged a look, and then they all ate in silence before her mother asked her, "So what did you do today?"

Charlotte swallowed her sigh, looking at her parents and then shrugging. "Just explored."

She would have to ask the ghosts what was going on, if they were still speaking to her.

"Not the Dark Woods, I hope," Simon said meaningfully before taking a sip of wine.

"No."

"Are you sure you're all right?" he asked, concern darkening his face.

No, I'm not. "I'm fine. How was the village?"

"A little depressing to be honest," Elizabeth said, casting a sidelong glance at Simon. "So many shops were closed. I know it's been tough, but I didn't realize how much."

Simon hmmed. "It is sad to see, but I suppose in some ways inevitable."

Elizabeth frowned at that. "I don't see why. It's a charming little village."

"One of many. They are, I'm afraid, common."

"But Greyswood is . . . different. It's *our* little village. I wish I'd known things were so bad here. I would have . . ."

"What?" Simon asked curiously as he set down his wine glass.

"I don't know. Something. You can't tell me you're okay with this, with your childhood village dying before your eyes."

"Actually," he said, earning both Charlotte's and Elizabeth's immediate attention, "it might make things easier in the long run."

Elizabeth's eyes narrowed. "Make what easier?"

Simon wiped his mouth with his napkin, placed it in his lap, and sat back in his seat. "I have been thinking of, considering, selling Grey Hall."

"What?"

His words hung in the air as they both stared at him in disbelief.

"You can't!" Charlotte could barely contain herself, her panic.

He held up a hand to stave off their objections. "Considering."

"Without discussing it? Simon." Elizabeth shook her head, clearly in shock at the revelation.

"I wanted to . . ." He paused gathering his thoughts. "I wanted to first see if it was even a viable option. I'm not sure of the market for such things."

"But—" Elizabeth cut in only for Simon to press on.

"And more importantly, I wanted to know how I truly felt about the idea before I mentioned it. My feelings about Grey Hall, as you both know, are complicated. I had hoped to try to come to terms with them before I broached the subject with you."

"Well," Elizabeth said a little tartly, "I'm against it."

"Me too."

Simon looked at them and sighed. "I thought as much. However, I would ask that you consider it." Elizabeth looked ready to argue some more but he hurried to add, "It is far too much for us, and we are here so seldom. It seems a waste. Please, take some time to think about it. Elizabeth?"

Her face was set, but she gave him a curt nod. Charlotte could hardly believe what she was hearing. Why wasn't her mom fighting for it? Why was he even thinking about it?

Nothing was right. Everything was wrong. A feeling of overwhelming panic began to well up inside her. He couldn't sell Grey Hall. He couldn't.

"Charlotte?" her father asked, pulling her from her careening thoughts.

"I . . . may I be excused?" she asked and then, barely waiting for her father's belated nod of assent, she bolted from the table.

She ran upstairs to her room and closed the door behind her. Suddenly, she felt foolish, but her emotions still roiled around inside her like a kettle coming to boil. Something was wrong. Something terrible was happening, but she couldn't put a name to it. Her parents must be enchanted by something. They weren't acting like themselves. And why couldn't they remember what she told them?

Had the ghosts done something to them?

She didn't know, but she was darn well going to find out.

CHARLOTTE FOUND HERSELF WANDERING the halls restlessly, until, somehow, her feet took her to the gallery. The Grey Hall portrait gallery was massive, with dozens and dozens of paintings hung high and low on the soaring walls. Walking down it was like walking through time. There was no adult portrait of her father and mother, and her dad had removed the Little Lord Fauntleroy painting with him in short pants the last time they were here.

She paused at the portrait of her grandparents, wishing she could have known them. Next was her dad's grandfather, Sebastian. He looked like a mix of mad scientist and turn-of-the-century explorer, wild hair and bright eyes shining at her from the flat canvas. She didn't recognize the next but then she saw Nicky—Sir Nicholas. He was even more handsome in the painting, standing with one foot on the bumper of a very fancy-looking, old-timey automobile, that same mischievous smile on his face. Down a few from Nicky was Ambrose, looking uncomfortable in his riding clothes and eyeing the dappled stallion next to him so warily she had to laugh.

A few more paintings down the hall, she recognized Sir Phineas. With his white wig, he seemed more like a king than a lord, she thought. Tall and broad and gripping the hilt of a sword, he glared at her ... imperiously. Charlotte smiled; her Word a Day calendar was certainly paying off. She took a step closer and studied the portrait. Phineas was an intimidating man, and ghost, but from this angle, she could swear there was just the hint of a smile at the corners of his mouth.

Near the end of the hall was a portrait that always made her shiver. She'd asked her dad about him the first time she'd seen the painting. He didn't tell her much—he wasn't much for Cross family history— but he knew the subject's name—Mordecai Cross.

Mordecai. Even the name was sinister. He had built Grey Hall out of the ashes of the previous house. He was tall like the others, and even more imposing than Phineas, but his face had none of the spark. It was harsh and cold. His mouth was a thin line set across the sharp edge of his jaw. His eyes were dark, almost black, and seemed to be looking straight into her soul. With a shiver, she walked on. Whatever answers she needed, she wasn't going to find them there.

Eventually, Charlotte made her way back down-stairs and let herself into the library. It was quiet and still.

"Hello?" she said softly, hoping the ghosts might reappear, but there was no response. "Are you there?" she asked a little more loudly.

She walked over to the bookcase the ghosts had come through and leaned in close to it, briefly wondering where ghosts hung out when they weren't walking through walls. Did they have a lounge or what? She added that to her Very Long List of questions for them if they ever reappeared. "Anybody in there?"

Still nothing.

She exhaled heavily in irritation. What was going on? Why couldn't her parents remember what she said? Why was her father thinking of selling Grey Hall? And why were there suddenly ghosts here? It was all wrong.

She nearly stomped her foot in frustration. She needed answers. Answers came in books, although she didn't have any idea what books to look in, so that idea wasn't much help.

She needed to learn more about the ghosts. Why were they stuck here? Why did Phineas seem so angry and then so defeated?

"Think, think, think," she told herself, chan-neling her inner Pooh.

Ghosts don't just hang around. Or do they? She really didn't know, and she doubted there'd be any book about *that* on these shelves. She needed to learn more about them, and maybe that would explain why they were stuck here, and what it had to do with her parents' weirdness.

There had to be a book in here about them. A family Bible, something that would give her some insight into who they were and what had happened to them. And unlike Ambrose, it wasn't just going to appear in front of her. It was time to start looking.

It took her nearly half an hour to find *The History of Grey Hall.* She climbed up the ladder, but it was on the shelf just above what she could reach. Not willing to be deterred, she stacked several large books on the top step of the spiral ladder and climbed back up, wobbling a little as she stood on tiptoes as she stretched to reach it.

"Do be careful."

Charlotte jerked around in surprise, nearly falling off the ladder—and would have if she hadn't managed to grab onto the bookshelf at the last moment. She turned to glare at whoever had interrupted her and was surprised to see Ambrose looking up at her, tugging worriedly on his hands.

"Ambrose," she scolded.

"I'm sorry. Are you all right?" he asked in a hushed whisper.

She huffed out a breath as she climbed back down. "I'm okay. I just need to reach that book." Then an idea occurred to her. She gave him the once over and then looked back up at the out-of-reach shelf. "You're taller than I am. Can you reach it?"

He shook his head sadly. "I cannot." He pushed his hand through the bookcase.

"You can't touch things?" she asked.

"I can if I concentrate, but I'm not the best at that. It's much more difficult than you would think—moving objects. It requires a great deal of energy."

Charlotte thought about that. It sort of made sense. But then, it sort of didn't. "Why don't you fall through the floor? You're walking on that."

He paused and looked down, then yelped and jumped before calming and giving a short laugh. "I don't know. Phineas probably does. He knows everything."

But Phineas wasn't there, and she needed help now. "But you know why you're stuck here, and what's going on with my parents, don't you?"

Ambrose blushed, as best as a ghost can. "Yes."

"Tell me. Please?"

He looked around the room anxiously, and her heart soared briefly before he shook his head. "I cannot."

"Why?"

"There are rules."

She didn't like that answer, but he didn't seem to have another to give her. She puffed out a breath of air in defeat, her lips fluttering against each other.

"Fine. I'll figure it out myself."

He beamed at that. "Do you think you can?"

"If you won't help me, what choice do I have?"

He looked from side to side and lowered his voice as if afraid he might be caught doing something he shouldn't. "I want to help."

"But Phineas won't let you."

"He's not a bad man, or wasn't—oh, ghost grammar is so confusing." Then he added with a worried frown. "It's just that he's been here the longest and has had his hopes dashed before. I don't think he could bear it again."

"I can do it. Whatever it is. I can do it," she promised, knowing it was foolish to promise something she didn't even understand.

"I believe you."

"But he doesn't?" she asked.

Ambrose shook his head.

"Then I'll just have to prove to him that I can."

His eyes brightened at her sureness and then dimmed. "But how?"

She chewed her lip in thought. "You can't tell me what's going on, and I can't tell my parents, or if I do they just forget it."

Ambrose brushed some ghostly lint off his floppy collar. "It makes one wonder why that is," he said trying to sound nonchalant.

"It's like we're cursed," she mused out loud.

His eyes went round, and a small gasp escaped his lips.

"We are cursed, aren't we?" she asked.

He clamped both hands over his mouth, and she turned away in thought.

"So, it is a curse. What is it?"

He removed his hands from his face but only shook his head helplessly.

"You can't tell me. Right," she said and put her mind back to thinking. "Back to where we started."

Ambrose's eyes drifted from her up to the book she'd been trying to get before.

"Are the answers in there?" she asked, but he could only shrug.

Rearranging the books again on the top step, she carefully climbed back up and just managed to get hold of the thick volume.

After she'd climbed back down, she blew the dust away from the cover, opened *The History of Grey Hall,* and started her search for answers in earnest.

CHAPTER FOUR

"SHE'LL BE ALL RIGHT," Elizabeth said as she pulled back the covers on Simon's side of the bed.

He released a breath as he shed his robe and climbed into bed next to her. He settled himself to sit against the headboard before turning toward her. "And you?"

She lifted her eyebrows in a shrug as she rolled onto her side. "Why didn't you tell me?"

"I . . ." he began but faltered. "I should have."

"Yes, you should have, but that's not what I asked. Why didn't you?" She thought they were well past this sort of thing.

He looked away, his forehead creasing as he tried to find the right words.

"I thought we didn't keep secrets from each other," she prompted, unable to keep the hurt from her voice.

"I am sorry. I didn't see it as keeping a secret. It's just that . . . I needed to work through how I felt about things before I discussed it with you." He glanced over at her, his expression softening. "You have quite an influence over me. I wanted to sort through my feelings first. Can you understand that?"

It was frustrating, but, yes, she could. She reached over, taking his hand. "I do."

And then she realized something. "Wilkes! I knew I recognized that name this afternoon on all those real estate signs in town. That's who called you this morning, isn't it?"

He sighed deeply. "Yes."

She was ready to let herself get wound up again, but he looked so forlorn, and she really did understand. With an effort, she pushed down her growing indignation and then let it go.

"It's all right," she told him.

"I am sorry for keeping you in the dark; that was not my intention. To be honest, I'm still not sure how I feel about it. I am . . . undecided."

She released his hand so she could sit up and scoot over close to him. His arm went around her shoulders, pulling her tightly to his side before relaxing his grip.

She leaned against his chest. "I know most of your memories of Grey Hall aren't exactly the picture-postcard variety."

He snorted.

"But they can't all be bad."

He was quiet for a minute before he shook his head. "Not all."

"And like it or not, this place isn't just your home, it's history. Your family's history. It's part of what makes you you."

He frowned, and she knew he believed that whatever hand Grey Hall had in the making of him it had not been for the better.

"The man I love. The man Charlotte adores," Elizabeth went on.

Her words pulled him from his melancholy, and he kissed the crown of her head.

"I don't want to lose any part of that," she finished.

"I had harbored the fanciful notion that you might be for it. Progress and all."

"Sometimes progress is good, but sometimes it's not. Sometimes we need to keep the past alive to remind us of where we've come from. But then I don't need to tell a time traveler that, do I?"

As he chuckled she could feel the vibrations in his chest.

She pulled slightly away from him. "I don't like the idea, but I promise you I will think about it."

He touched her cheek. "That is all I ask."

She rested her head against his chest again. She wasn't sure why the idea of losing Grey Hall bothered her so much. She'd been here fewer than a dozen times, but it was so . . . Simon. Losing it would be like losing a part of him. It was silly. It was just a house, a really honking big house, but still. Maybe it wasn't all about him if she was honest with herself.

She'd never had a home, not a real one, or at least one that she could remember. She and her father had lived in hotels most of her life, moving from town to town. The first real home she'd ever had was with Simon. The idea of selling a home, any home, and especially one like this with so many ties to the past, ties she'd always wanted and never had, made her feel oddly bereft.

But, she reminded herself, this wasn't about her. As much as she loved Grey Hall, this had been Simon's home, not hers. If he needed to let it go, she would find a way to accept that.

"OHH," CHARLOTTE SAID AS they arrived at the Christmas tree lot.

They'd had to drive several towns over to even find one. Greyswood used to have a fair selection, but there was not even one lot this year.

Pushing that thought aside, Simon let himself enjoy watching Charlotte as she dashed into the dirt lot forest of fir, spruce, and pine trees.

Both Charlotte and Elizabeth had been on the quiet side since his revelation at dinner last night. Their unnatural silence was . . . disquieting. As much as he relished the occasional peaceful moment, he yearned for the sounds of their nearly endless chatter and bubbling laughter.

"Has she said anything to you about . . .?" Simon asked as he and Elizabeth trailed behind her into the lot.

Elizabeth shook her head. "Not a peep."

Simon grunted. He would have preferred her to be vocal about it rather than keeping it inside. He would make a point to discuss it with her later.

"She was awfully quiet this morning at breakfast," he noted. "She looked—"

"Tired," Elizabeth finished for him. She glanced over at him, and he could see her emotions play across her face. Worry for Charlotte, and then worry for him followed by the desire to alleviate both. "She probably just stayed up late reading again."

Simon hmmed noncommittally.

"And I wonder where she gets that?" Elizabeth added with a wry smile.

He smiled at the thought, although he was still bothered by Charlotte's reaction to his news about potentially selling Grey Hall. Initially, she'd reacted as he'd expected: vehemently against it. Since that outburst, however, she'd not even mentioned it. That was very unlike her. Like her mother, she was not shy in expressing her opinions. The fact that she hadn't bothered him.

"Ohh, hot chocolate," Elizabeth said, spying a vendor's cart. "You want some?"

Simon declined, and while Elizabeth went to purchase some for her and Charlotte, he went in search of their child.

Simon found his daughter thoughtfully eyeing a very full Douglas fir. "Do you like it?" he asked.

"It's pretty," she said, sparing him a glance, "but there's no room for stuff."

She had a point. The tree was so dense that there was hardly a free spot to hang an ornament.

"What about a Noble or a Balsam?" he asked, gesturing to another part of the lot.

She pursed her lips in thought, squinting thoughtfully at the trees ahead. "Maybe."

"About what I said last night," Simon said suddenly, not planning on bringing it up now, but apparently needing to do so, "about—"

"Someone order a hot chocolate?" Elizabeth interrupted, and Charlotte stuck up her hand up in the air.

"Me!"

It was a little early for all that sugar, he thought, but the smile on her face as she took a warming sip kept that remark from finding its way out.

Elizabeth put her arm around Charlotte's shoulders. "Find anything good?"

"Maybe." Her eyes narrowed and with purpose in every step, she walked over to a Norway spruce. It was a little shaggy-looking but not too bad, or at least he thought so until he noticed that there was a rather noticeable hole on one side.

"I'm sure we can do better," he said.

"Doesn't it smell wonderful? Like Christmas!" Charlotte exclaimed.

The scent was a very pleasant pine, but . . . "We can do better," he said again.

"I love it."

"We're already getting a Charlie Brown tree," he noted. He was sure their usual Charlie Brown tree was little more than a branch that had been cut off, nailed to a stand, and sold at a premium. "There are dozens of more attractive trees here."

"It is a little wonky," Elizabeth admitted.

"I know," Charlotte said. "That's why it needs us."

"It needs us?" Simon asked, already knowing where this was headed.

Charlotte nodded vigorously and then looked at the tree adoringly. "No one else will buy it. It will sit here sad and lonely. The last tree on the lot."

She was overplaying her hand a bit, but Simon couldn't help but admire her for it.

"We could get an extra tree," Elizabeth offered.

"We already have plans for two."

"What's one more?" she replied with a smile.

He glanced at Charlotte, knowing it would be his undoing but unable to stop himself. "All right," he said with a sigh. "But I get to pick out the next one."

Charlotte grinned widely. "Thank you." And then she moved closer to the tree. "You're gonna love Grey Hall," she whispered to it.

He was doomed.

They spent the rest of the morning getting the trees situated. It was an absurdity—three Christmas trees crammed into a single drawing room—but the joy that filled the room told him that he'd made the right decision.

They decorated Charlotte's "wonky" tree that she'd nicknamed Bruce the Spruce with most of the ornaments Elizabeth had shipped from home. Many were handmade, although some were what he would describe as kitsch. No matter how much he protested, Elizabeth insisted on putting her "talking" Star Trek shuttle on the damn thing.

"It's vintage," she claimed. A disturbing thought for something from the 1990s.

He hung the slightly crumbling lacquered cookie wreath Charlotte had made when she was very young and stepped back to admire the tree. He'd tried to suggest that they turn the gaping hole toward the wall but had been summarily overruled.

"That's the best part," Charlotte told him as if he was very slow.

They all stood studying the tree and the gap before Elizabeth broke the silence.

"I have just the thing!" she said and rummaged around in a bag from their shopping yesterday. She pulled out a large, bespoke ornament in the shape of a man's face. "I was going to hang it on a door, but I think it's perfect here. What do you think, Charlotte?"

"Oh!" She walked over to admire it. "He's so . . . I don't know. Handsome in a leafy kind of way. Who is he?"

"The Green Man," Simon answered. "When did you get this?" he asked Elizabeth.

"In that shop in town—the Prince and the Pauper. You would have loved it," she told Charlotte. "All sorts of weird and wonderful things."

Charlotte ran her fingers over the carved wood center which had been cast in the shape of a man's face as if it had grown out of a tree. Leaves and berries were entwined for his hair and beard, making him look very much like he envisioned Tolkien's Ent looking when he was young.

"Who's the Green Man?" Charlotte asked.

"A legendary being who represents the cycle of death and rebirth. He's found in many different cultures but is primarily associated with Druids and now Pagans here in England. Depictions of him can be found dating back to the second century.

"As the legend goes, The Green Man has two sides—the Oak King who rules during summer and the Holly King who rules during winter. The transitions come on the solstices with the Holly King as the embodiment of the Green Man coming to power on the Winter Solstice to welcome the rising of the sun."

"Because it's the shortest day of the year?" Charlotte asked quite rightly.

"Precisely," Simon said proudly.

She admired the creation some more. "I think he's perfect."

Who was he to argue? "Do the honors."

Charlotte hung the Green Man in the empty space in the tree, and Simon had to admit it was fitting.

They continued decorating for another hour or so, finally working on his "perfect" tree. It was attractive, but even his attention was drawn to the others.

Once the last tree was finished, the rest of the Christmas festivities continued. He enjoyed a serenade of *All I Want for Christmas* that Elizabeth described as a "very Mariah Christmas" with the two of them lip-syncing along, though he was not completely certain it was a wholly appropriate song for his daughter to sing.

He was just starting to feel as though things were right in his world again when over lunch Charlotte suddenly asked a rather unnerving question.

"What do you know about Mordecai Cross?"

The question stopped him in his tracks. Mordecai was a name that he hadn't heard or thought of in years, and that was all for the better. The mere mention of that name as a child had made Simon shiver.

"Why do you ask?"

Charlotte shrugged with too-casual indifference. "Just wondering."

"Charlotte," he prompted.

"I was reading about him last night."

"What on earth made you do that?"

"Who's Mordecai?" Elizabeth chimed in. "Sounds scary."

"He was," Simon said. "Charlotte?"

Whatever her reasons for delving into the Cross family past, she was keeping them to herself. He wouldn't be surprised if he was to blame. His thoughts of selling Grey Hall could well have pushed her to it.

"When I was a child, his name was used to instill fear, which was quite successful. He was the original builder of Grey Hall in the early 1600s and, by all rights, a very unpleasant man."

"Do tell," Elizabeth quipped, earning a quelling look from Simon.

He considered carefully what he should say. He didn't know much, to be honest, but what he did know was distasteful.

"He was the worst sort of puritanical patriarch one could imagine. Cruel, unyielding, and singularly possessed by the belief that witchcraft would bring an end to civilization if left unchecked."

Elizabeth gave a low whistle.

"He committed heinous acts in the name of God, none of which we will ever discuss. He, like so much here, is better left dead and buried in the past."

Charlotte looked at Simon with an expression he could not quite decipher before nodding her head in acquiescence.

"Let us talk of more pleasant things, shall we?" he said.

"Agreed," Elizabeth said, clearly unsettled before recovering. "I have a question. Are we going to watch *Love Actually* tonight or tomorrow or both?"

HER FATHER HADN'T TOLD her anything she didn't already know. She'd fallen asleep again reading last night, but before she had she'd learned a little about Mordecai Cross, witch-hunter, and his devoutly religious wife, Sarah.

She hadn't even gotten to Phineas's time at Grey Hall. The book was detailed and, honestly, pretty boring. It started with the Norman Conquest and slowly inched forward from there. She would have skimmed ahead, but she wasn't sure what she was looking for. Anything could be important, though she doubted what some distant ancestor had done during the Second Barons' War or that one who was there when the Black Prince died in 1377 was all that significant to her current problem.

While her parents chatted and made plans for the coming days, Charlotte pushed her vegetables around her plate and made plans of her own. When they were otherwise occupied, she'd sneak back down to the library and see what else she could learn. Maybe Ambrose would even let a little something slip. She hated not knowing what was going on, although she had an uneasy feeling that when she found out, she might not be much happier.

CHAPTER FIVE

CHARLOTTE SETTLED HERSELF INTO THE window seat in her bedroom, *The History of Grey Hall* spread out across her lap. So far it hadn't been that helpful. It was clear that whoever wrote it . . . She checked the title page—Linton Allardf. Allardf? Well, old Mr. Allardf with an "f" must not have been much fun at parties because his book was as dry as a bone and, she was pretty sure, left out all the good stuff.

She was about to put it away when something outside the window caught her eye. She squinted against the glare of the lamp then cupped her hands over her eyes to shield them and leaned against the window.

It was that same owl!

It landed on the arbor again, stretched its wings, and then seemed to look right up at her. She opened the window, feeling a chill as the cold night air swept inside, and heard its distinctive screech. It was a chilling sound, somewhere between a cry and a shriek like a knife cutting metal.

It stared up at her, she was sure of it, and then it screeched again. It sounded crazy, but she could swear it was talking to her, calling to her.

She closed the window and hurried downstairs. It was already late. Her parents had retired to their rooms, but she still had to be quiet. She grabbed her coat and rummaged through a drawer for a flashlight. Finding a small one, she made her way out to the garden.

Not wanting to frighten the bird, she tucked the flashlight into her coat pocket and stepped outside into the cold winter night. She shivered and clutched her coat more tightly around her. It was dark, but there was just enough ambient light from the windows to see by. She stood just outside the door looking for the owl. It stood, quiet now, on its perch at the top of the arbor where during spring and summer honeysuckle and little white passionflowers bloomed. Right now, it was just a nest of dry branches—thin, spidery fingers clutching at the wood.

The owl swiveled its oval face to her and shrieked again.

"Hello," she said, slowly walking toward it.

The bird called again and flapped its wings. Charlotte felt her heartbeat pick up.

"Wait," she whispered, but it didn't.

The bird took off, seeming to hover in the air before sweeping gracefully away.

She followed a few more steps. "Don't go."

As if it heard her, the bird turned in the air, landing on the branch of a gooseberry bush that looked too delicate to hold its weight, but the branch didn't even bow.

Charlotte made her way out of the garden, easing the creaky gate open carefully, and walked until she was fewer than twenty paces from the bird.

"Have you come to visit?" she asked it.

The bird screeched again.

"I don't speak owl, but I wish I did."

The bird cried and then took off. Charlotte followed.

The moon was near three-quarters full, and the sky was clear. She didn't really need the flashlight to see by, and she didn't want to scare the owl, so she kept it in her pocket as she walked further away from the house.

The owl landed on top of a crumbling stone wall near the ruins of the original Grey Hall before calling to her again and then taking flight once more. As she caught up to it, it flew ahead, its tawny body a dark silhouette against the night sky.

It paused once more, turning back to her. The whole thing felt magical. It felt exciting. It felt . . . dangerous. Another shiver overtook her, but this one had nothing to do with the cold.

The bird screeched and took off once more, flying steadily this time, and she knew where it was going—the Dark Woods. She followed him for a few steps and then stopped. Something was compelling her to keep going, but something equally strong was holding her back. She stood there almost in mid-step, watching the owl disappear from view.

As soon as it was gone, the urge to follow it was gone as well.

She took several deep breaths, the air around her clouding with condensation.

That was super weird.

She took a few more settling breaths before turning to start back to the manor house. Strangely, it looked more like home than it ever had before. The chill of the night pushed her on, and the lights from the windows glowed warmly, invitingly.

The icy snow crunched under her feet as she trudged back to the house, and the uneasy feeling still lingered. She'd only gone a few steps when she saw something out of the corner of her eye. It was just a shadow, probably a branch caught in the wind, but . . .

She reached into her coat pocket, taking out the flashlight. She shined the light ahead, realizing whatever she'd seen had come from the old family graveyard. She tried to ignore the feeling of dread that washed over her at the realization and pushed out another breath. She'd already met three ghosts. Why was she scared of a little old graveyard?

She glanced back at the house, feeling the urge to get inside, but she needed to check out what she'd thought she'd seen. She took a hesitant step toward the graveyard and faltered.

Don't be a baby, she told herself and pressed on.

The iron gate didn't close properly anymore and stood slightly ajar. The low, pale stone wall surrounding it looked like piles of bones in the moonlight.

Don't be silly. Ghosts aren't so bad. Some are even kind of nice, she told herself.

Despite her pep talk, she stepped inside the gate tentatively. "Ambrose?"

There was no reply. She stepped further in and shined the light on the headstones. Mortimer Cross, Angelica Cross, Phineas Cross—

"Phineas!"

She walked closer to his monument. It was a bit like an obelisk with a large Celtic cross at the top. The only inscription was his name and the date of his birth and death—Christmas day three hundred years ago.

A sick feeling took root in her stomach, and she began to search the yard for Ambrose's and Nicky's markers. She found Ambrose first. He'd died Christmas Day two hundred years ago. She knew before she saw it what Nicky's would read.

All of them, all three of them, lords of the manor, had died on Christmas Day. She looked back at the house and toward the upper floor in the east wing where her parents' rooms were.

One hundred years apart.

Dad!

True fear suddenly clutching her heart, she raced back to the house, slipping in the icy snow, nearly falling in her haste. She ran inside, the door slamming back against its hinges as she threw it open. She stumbled on the stairs, skinning her knee but not caring. Her feet carried her as quickly as they could down the hall, and she burst into her parents' bedroom.

Her mother sat on the sofa, a book in her lap, her legs tucked beneath her while her father stood at the fire, jabbing it with an iron poker. When she burst in, they both looked at her with surprise. She stood there stupidly, gasping for breath and feeling suddenly absurd.

"Charlotte?" her mother asked in concern, hastily setting aside her book and coming toward her.

"What's wrong?" her father demanded, discarding the poker.

They both moved toward her, their eyes and mouths drawn tight in concern.

She panted for breath, unsure of what to say.

Her mother knelt down in front of her, taking her by the arms. "You're freezing." She cupped Charlotte's icy cheek with her warm hand. "Have you been outside?"

"What's happened?" her father asked anxiously as he led her toward the fire.

"I . . ." She didn't know what to say. "I thought I saw something outside and . . ."

"And you decided to go traipsing about in the dead of winter?" her father asked.

"In the middle of the night?" her mother added.

Her mother stripped off her coat and rubbed her arms before angling her to stand nearer the fire.

"What on earth has gotten into you lately?" her father pressed.

She wanted to tell them, but she knew they wouldn't remember even if she did. "I . . . I don't know."

Suddenly overwhelmed, she threw herself at her father, just needing to feel him, to know he was all right. He hesitated only a moment before wrapping his arms securely around her.

"It's all right, darling. It's all right," he soothed, but Charlotte knew it wasn't. She didn't know what was going on, but one thing she did know was that things were definitely not all right.

OVER BREAKFAST THE NEXT morning, Simon noticed that Charlotte was unnaturally quiet again. He glanced at Elizabeth, who silently shared his worry. Their happy, healthy, precocious child was drawn and sullen.

"Did you get some sleep?" he asked.

It took Charlotte a moment to look up from her toast, dry and untouched. "Hmm? Oh. Yeah, some. I'm sorry again about last night. I don't know what got into me."

Simon cast a worried look at Elizabeth again. Charlotte was nearly always bubbly, effervescent in the extreme. This morning, she was flat and lifeless. "You do know you can tell us anything."

She smiled at him, but it was pained and forced, making his heart ache.

"I know," she said, looking down at her untouched food. She seemed to come to a decision. "I'm okay."

She looked at him with more clarity than before, and he almost believed her.

"Really," she said before taking a bite of toast to prove her point but seeming to forget it was dry. She forced it down anyway. "Probably just hormones."

Simon couldn't stop a groan from escaping at that.

"I am *almost* a teenager," she said.

"Don't remind me."

He glanced once more at Elizabeth, arching an eyebrow in silent question and receiving only a shrug in reply.

Suddenly burdened by her usual appetite, Charlotte frowned at the toast. "Are there any eggs left?"

"I think so," Simon replied.

She walked over to the buffet and peered beneath the silver covers, humming happily to herself when she discovered the chafing dish with French toast.

With a sigh, Simon and Elizabeth shared a beleaguered look. God help him when she was actually a teenager.

Happily, and before that horrifying thought could take root further, Mr. Carter entered. "I am sorry to bother you, Sir Simon, but Mr. Wilkes is here."

"Here?"

"I can send him away if you prefer," Carter offered.

Simon hadn't been expecting the man, and it was rather forward to show up unannounced, but then he'd yet to meet an estate agent who wasn't bold, oftentimes too much so.

"I'll see him in the study," he replied before turning to Elizabeth. "Would you like to join us?"

"Definitely."

"Will you be all right?" he asked Charlotte, who was still busy piling food onto her plate.

"Maple syrup? Don't mind if I do," she said to herself. "Hmm? Oh, yeah, fine." Without turning away from the buffet, she waved at him over her shoulder.

Were all children this mercurial, he wondered with a sigh, or was he just lucky?

Ciarán Wilkes was a handsome man with a ready, perhaps too ready, smile. He flashed his teeth, so white they must have been veneers—no one in England came by those naturally—and strode forward.

"Sir Simon," he said in a gravely baritone that almost seemed to echo inside itself. "It's a pleasure to finally meet you." He shifted his charm to Elizabeth. "And you must be the Lady Cross."

"Must be," Elizabeth replied, shaking his hand politely, although Simon knew her body language well enough to know she was on guard.

Wilkes held up a rather expensive-looking gift basket. "I come bearing gifts."

It looked to be a fine selection of wines and cheeses. At least he'd gotten that right.

"Very kind of you," Simon said and then gestured toward the sofa.

"I won't take up much of your time," Wilkes said as he took a seat. "I just wanted to touch base and see this fine estate again."

"You've been here before?" Elizabeth asked.

"Years ago, although I never forgot it. I never forget a fine house."

"What is it we can do for you, Mr. Wilkes?" Simon asked.

"Ciarán, please. I really did just want to touch base, say hello face to face. I like to get a feel for the people I'm working for."

"You're not working for us yet," Elizabeth reminded him, and Simon couldn't quite keep the smile from his face.

"Quite right, although I'd like to change that. In my work, I see many great houses, but I see something special here. For all of Greyswood."

"I understand you've been buying properties in town," Simon remarked.

"Yes. My plans far exceed just Grey Hall, although that is the jewel in the crown. I hope to bring Greyswood into the twenty-first century. There are far too many villages like this one—neglected, left to a state of disrepair. I look at the sagging walls and the missing cobblestones and see possibilities. I see the future, and that future starts right here in Grey Hall."

CHARLOTTE CLOSED THE DOOR to her bedroom, sagging against it. Pretending everything was all right was exhausting. If only she could explain it all to her parents! They would know what to do.

But there was no point in that. No matter how she tried, they simply couldn't hold what she told him in their heads. She realized at breakfast that morning, however, that while they couldn't help, they could make it difficult for her to find out what was really going on. They might not understand the why, but they knew something was bothering her, and if they kept thinking that, they'd never leave her alone.

She'd spent the day with a cheery face, desperately trying to act normal, when all she could think about was last night and the danger her father was in. Or was he? She hated not knowing. She'd tried to summon the ghosts several times, but they never came. What if they never came again? The thought sent a wave of panic through her. How would she ever figure out what was going on without their help?

She glanced over at the little stack of books. She'd managed to sneak another one up to her room—the Cross family Bible—and hurried over to the window seat with it. It was heavy, and she put it down on the cushioned seat.

She turned to the back where the handwritten notes about births and deaths were scrawled on special pages. She skimmed over the lines, a ledger of her family history. Turning past births and baptisms, she came to deaths . . . and Phineas.

Phineas Aloysius Cross - Died Twenty-Five December 1721 - choked to death.

She swallowed hard and then pressed on.

Ambrose Clovis Morten Cross - Died Twenty-Five December 1821 - drowned.

That was hardly better.

Nicholas William Cross - Died Twenty-Five December 1921 - motor car accident.

How had her father never told her about that? Three ancestors dying on Christmas Day? He probably didn't know, she realized. He wasn't overly fond of the Cross family history, but three deaths exactly one hundred years apart? That felt like some family lore worth passing down from generation to generation. Or maybe it had been, and the curse had taken away the knowledge, or maybe no one liked to talk about it. Whatever the reason, Nicky had died in 1921, and this was 2021. Another chill overtook her.

A knock on the door shook her from her darkening thoughts, and her mother poked her head in. She stepped inside wearing a long midnight blue evening gown.

"We're heading to the Jacobs'. We won't be long, and the Carters are here if you need anything."

Her father appeared at her side, finishing tying his bow tie. "I don't see why we have to go."

Any other time Charlotte would have smiled at her father's predictable complaint but not tonight.

"They invited us."

"But we don't like the Jacobs."

"*You* don't like the Jacobs," she replied. Her mother turned back to her. "We won't be late."

Remembering she had a role to play—be happy!—Charlotte told them to stay out as long as they wanted.

"Eat, drink, and be merry," she ordered them, pretending to raise a glass in a toast.

Her father raised an unamused eyebrow at her.

"Have some hors d'oeuvres for me!"

Her father sighed before giving her a wan smile. "See you soon, darling. Emphasis on soon," he muttered as they left.

She put the book aside and hurried to the closed door. Pressing her ear to it, she listened carefully. She could hear her father complaining about someone named Bronwyn and her wandering hands and her mother's answering laugh as they headed down the hall.

After a moment, she eased the door open and silently slipped down the hall after them. She watched from a hidden corner of the upper landing as they headed out for the evening. Waiting until she was sure they were in the car and driving away, she snuck downstairs and back into the library.

She walked a few paces into the room. "Ambrose?"

There was no answer, but this time she was not going to take silence for an answer.

"I know you're here or near at least and that you can hear me."

A head poked through the bookcase, and Charlotte sighed with relief. "How do you know that?"

"Ha! I didn't. Please come out."

Chagrined, Ambrose walked through the bookcase. "You're very sneaky."

"Thank you. Now, would you please explain to me what's going on?"

He hesitated, and that just made her more agitated. She began to pace.

"Last night I saw an owl—"

"Y-you did?"

"In the garden."

He looked wistful. "Oh, I do so miss the garden," he said, off track again. "They say I had a way with flowers."

"Ambrose," she said, stopping and turning to him. "The owl. What does it mean? I saw it before, and last night it was like it was . . . calling to me."

"Oh dear. Oh dear, oh dear, oh dear."

"Ambrose."

He looked stricken. "This is not good. Or is it?" He tugged on his chubby fingers anxiously. "I wish I was brighter," he said finally. "I never was very good at these sorts of things."

"You've seen the owl then?" she asked.

He nodded. "In the garden from the windows."

"What does it mean?"

"It means, my dear," Phineas said, striding through the bookcase, "that I have underestimated you."

She sighed in frustration. "And what does *that* mean?"

"Don't be tart. It is most unbecoming," he replied.

She managed—barely—to school her emotions. "Will you please tell me what is going on? Why did you three all die on Christmas Day? What or who is that owl and is . . . is my father in danger?"

"The former is complicated," he said cautiously, "and as to the latter, I am sorry to say, yes. Unless we find ourselves a miracle, your father will suffer the same fate as we. Three days hence, on Christmas Day, he will join us beyond the veil."

CHAPTER SIX

"**D**IE?" CHARLOTTE CHOKED.

"I believe that is what I said," Phineas replied.

"Technically, you said 'join us beyond the veil,'" Ambrose added, doing a passable impression of Phineas.

"It means the same thing," Phineas spat out.

Charlotte ignored their argument, trying to process what he'd just told her. Her father was going to die. In three days, he was going to die unless they found a miracle.

She felt sick, physically sick to her stomach, and her cheeks suddenly burned. A rising sense of panic threatened to overwhelm her at the mere thought of it, but she caught herself. She had to keep her head. She had to think logically. It's what he'd do. *Clear heads make good choices*, her father's voice echoed in her head.

Then a tiny spark of hope flared in her chest. She'd seen miracles before. She would find the one needed to save her father. She would.

"What sort of miracle do we need?"

"What sort?" Phineas asked. "What in blazes do you think, girl? The sort that will break the curse."

"So it is a curse."

"What else would it be?"

Why was he being such a pill? "Why didn't you tell me?"

He glared at her, and she was reminded again of the similarity between him and her father. She put that thought squarely out of her mind.

"Because I did not think you would be able to help! Why do you think?"

"How can you expect someone to help you if you won't even tell them what's wrong?"

He was about to offer a rude reply when Nicky sauntered through the bookcase. "What's Cinemax After Dark, and do you think the Carters might subscribe?"

"Nicholas," Phineas ground out. "The child is here."

"Oh. Oh! Sorry," Nicky said with a slight blush of his pale cheeks. "I was watching television with the Carters, and—"

"*With* the Carters?" Charlotte asked.

"Oh, they don't know I'm there, and they don't watch very often. More's the pity."

"Being a ghost is rather lonely," Ambrose explained.

"It is torture," Phineas added. "Forced to walk these halls unseen for centuries. Able only to speak to one soul every hundred years." He cast a glare in Ambrose's direction.

"I said I was sorry. I didn't mean to manifest and be seen. I was overly excited."

"And I'm the one this time," Charlotte confirmed.

"Yes," Phineas sighed, clearly not too keen on the idea. He turned to look at her, narrowing his eyes. "Although, you've gotten farther than the other two."

"The other two?"

Ambrose smiled kindly. "The last two souls we revealed ourselves to. Phineas's grandson Nigel—"

"Corn-faced simpleton," Phineas grunted.

"And Nicholas's father Andrew, who..." Ambrose paused, trying to find the right words.

Nicky supplied them for him. "Was too drunk to find his own backside much less help." He smiled at Charlotte. "You are my first. And I must say, I'm very glad it's you."

Charlotte blushed at that but quickly refocused on the task at hand.

"So you died," she said, looking at Phineas, "in 1721. Choking, it said."

"On a chicken bone," Nicky said with a laugh that earned him a searing look from Phineas.

Charlotte turned to Ambrose. "And you drowned?"

Ambrose sighed. "I did."

"Yes," Phineas said with mock pride, "managing a feat few can claim—drowning in a mere three inches of water."

Ambrose's cheeks, already red, grew a shade darker. "I was hunting turnips and slipped. Fell into a stream. It could have happened to anyone."

Nicky snorted. "Not anyone."

"Well, at least I wasn't murdered by my own creation."

That got Charlotte's attention.

"I was killed in a dignified manner," Nicky said hastily. "In a motor car accident."

"I'm sorry," Charlotte said sincerely, looking at each of them.

Phineas seemed moved by her remark before he pushed the emotion aside. "We do not dwell upon that we cannot change. Death comes to us all. But this," he said, gesturing vaguely, anger tightening his eyes, "this imprisonment . . . it is intolerable."

"It's all part of the curse, isn't it?"

"Yes."

"Then it's simple. We'll break it. We'll break the curse, and you'll be free, and my dad'll be safe."

"Oh, child, if only it were so simple," Phineas said with unexpected softness.

"There's got to be a way. If it can be done, it can be undone." Charlotte didn't know what it would take, but she would do anything to save her father.

"And you thought she was 'just a girl,'" Nicky said with a broad smile.

"Words are not deeds," Phineas replied, but she saw a glimmer of hope in his eyes that was not there before.

ELIZABETH SHOULDN'T HAVE TAKEN pleasure in Simon's tight smile as he danced with Lucinda Delacourt, but she couldn't help herself. As the local baronet, he was in high demand. He'd been a good sport about it all so far, even enduring a dance with handsy Bronwyn Edgecomb, although Elizabeth had to give the old girl credit—Bronwyn was pushing eighty and still managed to cop a feel.

As Simon turned Lucinda around the small dance floor in the Jacobs' ballroom, he glared at Elizabeth as they drifted by. There would be hell to pay later, she thought.

Despite Simon's understandable aversion to things like this—he didn't like being the center of attention unless he was standing at a lectern—the party was enjoyable. Part of her was still worried about Charlotte; the girl was not herself. But, having been a preteen girl herself, Elizabeth knew there could be a hundred and one different reasons for her mood shifts. She wasn't exactly crazy about the idea of her having gone out in the middle of the night though, not that Grey Hall was exactly in a bad neighborhood. It wasn't in any neighborhood unless you counted their closest neighbors to the south, and they were several miles away.

It must have been lonely for Simon as a boy. She knew he'd spent most of his childhood away at school or at his grandfather's home in Hastings if he could, but still. As an only child, there must have been times when he was the only one rattling around the mansion. His parents weren't bad people, but they were distant and apparently unequipped to deal with a child, especially one as brilliant as Simon. He had been conceived to continue the Cross name and little else. At least, that's what he believed. In the end, it didn't matter what the truth was, those thoughts were heavy burdens for any child.

Charlotte would never feel that way. They both made sure of that.

A waitress appeared at her shoulder with another round of canapés. It was a good thing because

Elizabeth was absolutely starving. Appetizers only gave her an appetite.

"Oh, those look good," she said as she took a small cocktail napkin from the server's tray and eyed the offering.

"Lamb and pomegranate stuffed persimmons," the woman explained.

Now, that was not your usual Christmas fare, and she was here for it.

Browned lamb was dotted with deep red pomegranate seeds and stuffed inside half of a reddish-orange persimmon. She could smell the sage and other spices as she took one from the tray.

The food had been fantastic and unusual so far. Goose Rumaki, Baked Brie and Cranberry Bites, Spiced Crab Apples, and a warm, spicy drink with a bit of a kick that Simon informed her was called Wassail, after the Yule tradition where young women would go "wassailing" or visiting their neighbors to spread the cheer of the season.

"These are amazing," she said. Before she'd even finished chewing, she took another. Miss Manners would not have approved, but Elizabeth didn't care. These were divine.

"Who made these?"

"Miss Prince," the serving girl said with a nod to the kitchen.

"Fiona Prince?" Elizabeth asked. "The one who owns The Prince and the Pauper in Greyswood?"

"Yes, ma'am."

The server left to move on to more guests before Elizabeth could take the tray from her and eat them all.

Elizabeth stuffed what was left of the second persimmon into her mouth and delicately dabbed at the corners of her lips with the cocktail napkin, smiling at a couple passing by.

She'd been accepted; well, they'd accepted that they had to accept her, an American as Lady Cross, but only a few of them bothered to hide their displeasure. She glanced back at the dance floor. Meanwhile, Simon was the most popular thing going.

Serves him right for thinking of selling Grey Hall. Although it certainly hadn't helped her cause that Mr. Wilkes had made a compelling argument that it was time for Grey Hall and Greyswood to embrace the future. She knew Simon wanted to do that, not embrace the future so much as leave the past in the past, but she wasn't so sure it was the right thing for the town or for him—not that she got to dictate what was right for either of them.

Another tray, this time with what looked and smelled like mini butternut squash tarts passed by. *Yum.*

Although she didn't know her well at all, Elizabeth loved the idea that Fiona's creativity didn't end at the shop. The food tonight was surprising and so unique. Having worked part-time waitressing at catering gigs in college, Elizabeth knew caterers seldom got the credit they deserved and decided to give her compliments to the chef personally.

Without giving a thought to Miss Manners or watchful eyes, she asked one of the serving girls how to get to the kitchen.

She found Fiona sending out a fresh wave of goose.

"Those are incredible," Elizabeth said, watching the trays pass by, barely managing to keep her sticky fingers off them.

"Thank you—Oh! Hello," Fiona said pleasantly. "Elizabeth, isn't it?"

"You run a store and you cater stunning parties?" Elizabeth asked and then made a show of looking behind Fiona. "Where's your cape?"

Fiona laughed. "If working two jobs makes someone a superhero then half of England is an Avenger."

Elizabeth eyed another platter of appetizers ready to make the rounds. "The food is really, really good. Different."

Fiona smiled enigmatically. "It's based on Yule and Winter Solstice more than traditional Christmas fare. I believe Mrs. Jacobs thought it was . . . edgy."

Elizabeth laughed before sneaking a rogue bit of brie. "Well, edgy or not, it's terrific."

"Thank you."

One of the servers came back, nearly colliding with Elizabeth in her haste.

"I'm so sorry, Lady Cross, I didn't see you," the girl said before taking a fresh tray and hurrying off.

"Lady Cross?" Fiona asked, and Elizabeth saw the dawn break. "You're that Elizabeth. I should've known." Her open expression suddenly closed.

Elizabeth was troubled and disappointed. At home, no one knew or cared about her husband's title. She wasn't used to the social barriers it sometimes erected here. She forced a questioning smile to her face.

"Is that a bad thing?"

Fiona hesitated and then sighed. "No. I'm sorry. Old habits die hard, I'm afraid."

"Not a fan of the Crosses?" Elizabeth guessed. When Fiona hesitated, she rushed ahead, giving them both an out. "Don't get me wrong. Simon is the bee's knees, but I know some of his ancestors . . ." She grimaced in sympathy.

Fiona laughed. "No, it's nothing like that. I . . . it's silly really."

"I love silly," she replied.

Fiona frowned and busied herself wiping down the counter before sighing again. "I shouldn't have said anything. It really is ridiculous."

"Even better."

Fiona lost a battle with a smile and then sighed heavily, her shoulders rising and then falling with some unseen weight. "All right, but don't blame me when you think less of me after you hear it."

She paused again, gathering her thoughts before continuing. "It's ancient history now, but . . . many years ago, hundreds of years ago, your—an ancestor of your husband's treated one of mine . . . rather poorly."

"How poorly?"

"Killed her, we think."

"Oh." That was not what she was expecting and was suddenly at a loss for words. "That's . . . not good. I'm sorry."

Fiona smiled graciously. "It's hardly your fault, and it's beyond absurd that it still bothers me. It's just that—well, being different is never easy, and it certainly wasn't four hundred years ago."

"What happened?" Elizabeth asked, but before Fiona could reply, the hostess swept into the kitchen.

"You simply must send out more goose," she said. "They're positively clambering for more. Oh! Lady Cross? What are you doing in here?"

Elizabeth cast a quick glance at Fiona, knowing that their conversation had to end but wishing it didn't.

"I just came in to tell Fiona how wonderful the food was," she said.

"It is, isn't it?" Amelia said delightedly. "Now, more goose!" she added to Fiona before taking Elizabeth by the arm and leading her out. "My cousin Hadrian is positively *dying* to meet you."

"We wouldn't want that," Elizabeth said, casting a final glance over her shoulder as she let herself be shanghaied, but she wasn't done with Fiona Prince yet.

"How did it start?" Charlotte asked. "The curse?"

Phineas took a deep breath, and Nicky said, "You might want to sit down. He tends to be long-winded."

Phineas shot him a withering look before turning back to Charlotte. "I shall be brief for there is, unhappily, very little of which we are certain."

"Tell her about the witch!" Ambrose said excitedly.

"Spoilers!" Nicky quipped.

"I was getting to that," Phineas said irritably.

Ambrose took a step back and gestured theatrically for him to continue.

Phineas cleared his throat. "As I was saying, there is scant we are certain of regarding the origin of the curse. What we do know," he added before Ambrose could interrupt him again, "is that four hundred years ago, our dear progenitor, Mordecai—"

"A real git," Nicky added.

Phineas closed his eyes to keep from losing his temper. "Mordecai," he continued in a slightly strained voice, "committed some . . . act against a woman he claimed to be a witch."

"I think the evidence shows he was right," Nicky said and then added after Phineas's glower, "Well if she was just a farmer's wife we wouldn't be in this predicament, would we?"

"He's got a point there," Ambrose said but then hastily continued, "not that it excuses what he did. Whatever it was precisely."

"Mordecai was a witch-hunter like Matthew Hopkins," Charlotte said.

Nicky's grin was so large it split his face. "I told you she was special."

"We saw a documentary about him at school."

"That is somehow deeply disturbing," Nicky replied.

"If you are finished," Phineas ground out. "Yes, he was a witch-hunter. An unfortunate avocation, but, given the times, not all that surprising. Such foolishness."

"What did he do to her? The witch, I mean," Charlotte asked worriedly.

"Those details remain . . . obscured. However, I feel it is safe to assume that whatever he did resulted in the poor woman's death."

Phineas eyed her carefully, seeming to weigh how she took in this particular piece of information.

Charlotte wrapped her arms around herself, feeling suddenly cold. "He killed her?"

Phineas looked at her intently. "You suffer from a chill?" he asked gently before glaring at the empty fireplace. "What sort of laggards has your father hired? Why is there no fire in the hearth? Thoroughly unacceptable—"

"I'm all right," Charlotte said, forcing herself to relax her arms. It was all just a little overwhelming. Her great, great, so-many-greats-she-wasn't-sure grandfather had murdered someone, and now her father might die because of it.

No. She wasn't going to let that happen.

She raised her chin. "What was the woman's name?" If she was going to find out what happened, she was at least going to need to know that.

She thought she saw something akin to pride flash in Phineas's eyes before he replied. "Elara. Elara Prynce."

CHAPTER SEVEN

"Elara," Charlotte whispered to herself. That was the name of the witch—the woman. "Do you know anything about her?"

Phineas paced uneasily back and forth across the library. "Very little, I am afraid. She was a village woman—there are very few accounts of her that I was able to discover. She kept to herself, believed in the old ways."

"The old ways?" Charlotte asked.

"Pagan. Herbs and such. There was one story of her curing a boy in the village of the sweating sickness."

"Influenza," Nicky added helpfully, earning a fleeting scowl from Phineas for interrupting his narrative.

"Yes. She was unfortunate enough to attend the birth of a stillborn child. Rumors began to circulate that she had traded the child's life to Satan in return for her powers."

"That's ridiculous," Charlotte said. "Witches, even back then, weren't Satan worshippers."

Phineas arched an eyebrow at her statement but continued. "Be that as it may, there was a fever upon the land at the time. King James VI was consumed by thoughts of the supernatural. He even wrote a book—*Daemonologie*—delving into the dangers of witchcraft and demonic magic. The fear grew so quickly across the country that Parliament passed a statute making witchcraft punishable by death."

He paused and took a deep breath. "You are far too young to realize this yet—and I am sorry that you must now—but petty men, small men, will always find a way to force someone beneath them, to find an outlet for their self-hatred."

He grimaced, although she wasn't sure he was still thinking about the witch-hunters.

Clearing his throat, he continued. "Mordecai Cross was one such man."

Charlotte tried to take all of that in. It was one thing to read about history in a history book or see a documentary, but it was another to have your own flesh and blood relative responsible for something so . . . awful.

Then something occurred to her. "But why Christmas? If she was pagan, why choose that day?"

Phineas's eyes shifted to her, and for the second time she thought she saw a flash of pride move across his face. "That is a very good question. One I do not have an answer for."

He seemed to lose himself in thought briefly before drawing up to his formidable height. "You said that you saw an owl earlier. Is that correct?"

"Yes."

"Did it try to lead you to the Dark Woods?"

She thought about it. "I think so."

"You mustn't follow it. I fear it is not a bird at all."

"We don't know that—" Nicky put in.

"How many four-hundred-year-old owls do you know?" Phineas replied sharply. Nicky made a face.

"If it's not a bird," Charlotte ventured cautiously, "it's . . .?"

"The witch's familiar: an imp, a spirit."

Charlotte pictured the owl. It had looked a little strange and, now that she thought about it, the branch it rested on didn't bow at all under its weight.

"How do you know?"

"I was uncertain at first, but it leaves no footprints in the snow, nor has it changed in all these years. It is not so great a leap of logic." He grew quite serious and declared, "You must not follow it."

"Shouldn't I though? I've heard stories about the Dark Woods since I was little . . ." That earned an impolite snort from Phineas, who had the good grace to look abashed and gave her a slight bow of apology, waving her on. "… that a witch haunts the woods. Unless there's another witch wandering around, it's got to be Elara."

"Precisely why you should avoid it."

Charlotte paused for a moment to arrange her argument before continuing.

"But if I'm going to break the spell, I'm going to have to, aren't I? I mean, if she's the one who cast the curse, then shouldn't I go ask her to undo it?"

"Ask her? Dear child, she is a witch."

"So? Witches are people."

He seemed briefly thunderstruck by that announcement before conceding the point. "I suppose that is true, in its way, however that does not mean she is not dangerous." He gestured to the Nicky and Ambrose. "I believe we are evidence enough of that."

Charlotte knew that was true, and the witch might hate her as much as she hated Mordecai. She was a Cross, after all, but could she break the curse without facing her?

Phineas was watching her carefully, the same way her father did when he was worried she was about to do something reckless.

"You must be careful," Ambrose said gently. "Promise us you will be?"

"I will," she promised without thinking, and she would be, as much as she could. "What else can you tell me about the curse? Is there anything—"

The door to the library opened, interrupting her, and all three ghosts turned to the door warily.

Elizabeth poked her head in, leaned back out, and then called, "She's in the library."

Her mom looked amused as she stepped inside. "How did I know?"

When her father came in a few seconds later, Ambrose scrambled across the floor and ducked down behind a large reading chair and peeked up over the top of it, earning an eye roll from Phineas.

Nicky walked slowly toward Elizabeth. "You woefully undersold the new Mrs. Cross, dear Ambrose. She is lovely."

Charlotte frowned as the younger ghost circled her mother, looking at her with undisguised admiration. It was an expression that mimicked the one her father so often wore.

For once, though, Simon wasn't admiring his wife. He was looking around the room with an odd expression on his face.

"What's wrong?" Elizabeth asked.

"Nothing," father and daughter replied in stereo, earning Charlotte a curious look from her father.

Elizabeth laughed and focused on her husband. "What's gotten into you?"

For a moment, Charlotte thought her father could see Nicholas, but his eyes didn't land on anyone or any particular thing or person. They just scanned the whole of the room warily.

His pinched look didn't recede. "I'm fine."

"Interesting," Phineas observed as he walked closer to Simon. He reached out and waved a hand through Simon's body.

Her father tensed, repressing a shudder. "It's rather cold in here, isn't it?"

"Very interesting," Phineas said, continuing to study his descendant.

"You're not helping," Charlotte said under her breath.

"Not helping with what, sweetie?" Elizabeth asked as she walked right through Nicky, who appeared ready to make a quip but was silenced by a piercing look from Phineas.

"The ghosts," she said offhandedly, hoping that it might stick this time.

"The ghosts? Are—" Her mother's expression changed in an instant, going briefly blank before resuming her previous mild curiosity. "Not helping with what, sweetie?"

"Just some research," Charlotte said, trying not to sound too defeated.

"Research?" her father said, instantly interested.

She should have known better.

"About what, darling?"

Uncle Jack had taught her that the best lies were usually thin versions of the truth. "Family history. Grey Hall. That sort of thing."

Happily, this was one area of research her father was not overly interested in.

"Ah."

Meanwhile, Ambrose had overcome his shyness and emerged from his hiding place. Cautiously, he tiptoed toward her father. He waved a hand in front of his face to confirm he remained unseen and then began to do a little jig.

"Did you have fun at the party?" Charlotte asked, trying not to laugh and doing her best to ignore Ambrose's antics.

"I did," Elizabeth said and then frowned. "Are you sure you're all right?"

Charlotte bit her lip to keep from reacting. "I'm fine. Just tired."

Ambrose kept reaching through her father's chest and wiggling his fingers. It was disconcerting. She glanced over at Phineas, silently pleading with him to control the others.

He strode over to Ambrose and grabbed him by the scruff of the neck. "That's enough, you great, galloping gollumpus." He shoved Ambrose toward the bookcase, signaling for Nicky to follow suit, before turning back to Charlotte. "Until tomorrow, my dear."

He gave her a small bow before he and the others disappeared.

"Charlotte?" her father asked, a crease of worry at his eyes.

"Sorry, I was just thinking. What do you know about the witch in the Dark Woods?"

From his startled expression this was the last thing he'd expected her to say. He gathered himself and came toward her. "Very little, and nothing that will be discussed at this hour."

"But—"

He held up a hand to forestall her pouty-faced begging. "Not tonight."

Her mother's smile smoothed the hard edges of his words.

"Tomorrow?" she asked with a cheeky smile.

Her father snorted and gave a short laugh. "Possibly."

Charlotte knew that meant yes and grinned.

Simon sighed. "All I know is that I need to take off my shoes. It's not easy being the belle of the ball," he said, winning a laugh from both mother and daughter.

CHARLOTTE DIDN'T WANT TO go to town; she wanted to talk to Phineas. She'd tried to summon him that morning, but he didn't come, and then her mother had cornered her, insisting that she come to town with her.

Charlotte had almost pretended she was sick to try to get out of it, but that was about the only thing that would put her under a microscope more than she already was. She knew she wasn't acting like herself, not herself at Christmas anyway. She suppose, for a few hours at least, she could play along, and then she could sneak off and find Phineas again.

"Where are we going?" she asked, trying to sound cheerful about it.

"A new store in town."

"I thought you said everything was closed."

"Not everything. Besides, I want you to meet someone. I think you'll find her interesting."

"Who?"

"Patience, grasshopper."

A few minutes later, they parked out front of the Prince and the Pauper, which was definitely not like any of the other stores in town. It was filled with wonderful, creative little things.

"Fiona?" Elizabeth called out as they stepped inside, the bell overhead announcing their arrival.

A pretty woman about her mom's age appeared near the back of the store, a smile blossoming on her face. "Elizabeth? Or should I say—"

"Elizabeth, please."

"I wasn't sure you'd want to talk. I was so rude to you, I . . ." She trailed off as she noticed Charlotte. "Hello."

"Charlotte, this is Fiona Prince. Fiona, this is my daughter."

"Hi," Charlotte replied, gazing at a statue of a man made entirely of woven branches. "I love your store."

"Thank you. Can I get you some tea or something? It's cold today, isn't it?"

"No, we're fine. Thank you. I was wondering though if you'd tell me about that ancestor of yours."

Charlotte perked up at that.

Fiona cast a quick, uncertain glance in Charlotte's direction. "I'm not sure it's . . ."

"Oh, it's all right," Elizabeth assured her. "She loves history. The gorier the better."

"She's not wrong," Charlotte said with a bright smile.

Fiona still looked a little unsure.

Unsure usually meant it was a "grown-up topic," which immediately piqued her interest. Charlotte pulled out her best "Please?"

Fiona studied her briefly and then sighed in capitulation. "All right. Well, as I was saying last night. It's silly really."

"Apparently," Elizabeth put in, "one of your father's ancestors did something very bad to one of hers."

"Really?" Charlotte asked, intrigued now.

Elizabeth gave a soft laugh. "You see what I mean?"

Charlotte scowled at her, but it was a tepid version of her father's and was met only with another laugh.

"What happened?" Charlotte asked.

"Well," Fiona said, seeming to warm to the idea of telling the tale, "four hundred years ago, give or take, one of my ancestors was thought to be a witch."

She paused to let that nugget sink in, clearly expecting them to be shocked or scoff at the idea. However, her mother merely nodded, and Charlotte looked at her expectantly, trying to keep her face looking politely interested while insides were having a complete spaz.

"A witch?" Charlotte said, hope flaring in her chest.

"That's the story anyway. And supposedly, she was celebrating Winter Solstice or Yule, and the lord of Grey Hall wasn't too keen on the idea."

"Mordecai," Charlotte said almost to herself.

Fiona looked at her with a puzzled expression. "Yes. Mordecai Cross. How did you know?"

"She's a student of history," her mother said proudly. "And she's nosy."

Charlotte felt herself blush at both statements for different reasons but pushed her feelings aside. "He was a witch-hunter."

Whether Fiona was surprised at the bluntness of that or that it was a child that had said it, Charlotte didn't know and didn't care. She was used to adults being surprised at what she knew.

"What did he do?" Charlotte asked intently, praying for some bit of information that might help her save her father.

Fiona glanced at Elizabeth before continuing. "Well, according to the family lore, he . . . killed her."

"How?"

Fiona's eyebrows rose and then she fought down a smile. "You weren't kidding," she said to Elizabeth before answering Charlotte's question. "He . . . drowned her."

"Awful," Elizabeth said softly.

"I believe back in the day," Fiona went on, "it was a fairly common test to see if the person was a witch or not. Bind them and then toss them in the water. If they sank, they were innocent. If they floated, lucky them, they were deemed a witch and killed."

"Heads I win, tails you lose," Elizabeth said.

"Exactly."

Charlotte's mind was racing now. "Do you know where it happened?" she asked, trying not to sound too interested, but inside she was as tense as she could be.

"I'm not sure. I've always assumed somewhere in the Dark Woods. At least that's what she haunts now, or so the stories go."

"If it's any comfort," Elizabeth said, "everyone has ancestors who've done horrible things." Her face creased. "And that really shouldn't be a comfort, but you know what I mean."

"Did she ever curse anyone?" Charlotte blurted out, speaking before she thought.

"Charlotte!" Elizabeth said with surprise in her voice. She turned to Fiona apologetically. "I'm so sorry. I know this is a sensitive subject for you."

Fiona smiled in understanding. "It's silly that it still bothers me. I didn't know her, obviously, it's just . . ." She finished with a shrug.

"I get it. Not to mention, the Cross family hasn't always been exactly the warmest and fuzziest bunch in town," Elizabeth said.

Fiona laughed. "No, but that looks like it's changing," she added hopefully.

"I'd like to think so."

"I think it has," Fiona said sincerely. "I just hope the village sticks around long enough to see it."

"It's really that dire, isn't it?"

"I'm afraid so. Things are in such a state of disrepair, we've lost just about all of our tourism. The hotel needs work and the pub. Not to mention the historical sites are . . . well, they haven't been kept up at all—the old church, the folly, the standing stones, and the holy well. The town just doesn't have the money."

Disappointed she didn't get an answer to her question and couldn't ask *more* questions without drawing unwanted attention, Charlotte tuned out as her mother and Fiona discussed the state of the village. Her thoughts were somewhere else, somewhere she needed to go—the Dark Woods.

She barely remembered the extra decorations they'd bought or the drive home. She did her best to feign interest and keep her mom from catching on that something was bothering her. If she did, she'd never get away, and she *needed* to get away.

It took nearly three hours for Charlotte to get away. Her mother and father finally had some "estate business" to deal with and left her alone, at least until dinner.

The late afternoon wintery sky was a sheet of depressing gray. Fitting, she supposed. Putting on her heaviest coat and gloves, she wrapped a scarf around her neck before she started off toward the Dark Woods. It seemed to get colder with each step.

When she finally reached them, she stood at the edge, looking anxiously at the dense forest of oak, thorn, and rowan.

"You got this," she told herself and then took a step in.

Part of her expected to feel something when she crossed the threshold, some tingle of magic or something, but she didn't feel any different. Emboldened, she walked deeper in.

The woods were well named. They *were* dark. The trees were clustered so close together that they created a canopy overhead blocking out what little light there was. Because of the low light and overcast sky, shadows were no more than dull outlines against a forest floor covered with dead leaves and fallen branches.

She nearly tripped on the exposed root of a huge tree, and remembering both her father's and Phineas's warnings slowed her steps. The quiet was oppressive, punctuated by the sound of a distant rustle of leaves or the cry of a fox in the distance. Thankfully, the woods were big but not that big. She could probably get lost; probably was, she thought as she turned around—it did all look the same—but if she plotted a straight-line course, she'd find her way out eventually.

Small dried branches and leaves crunched under her feet, unnaturally loud in the stillness around her. Swallowing down her trepidation, she pressed on until she caught sight of what looked like what had once been stone wall. She followed the remnants of it until she came to a natural hollow covered with deep green moss, one of the few bursts of color in an otherwise muted world. The ground of the hollow seemed to be sinking in on itself. At the far side of the mossy crater were more stones. Some were piled on top of each other, while others had long ago fallen, and were now partially swallowed by the forest floor.

She was about to take a step toward it when she heard a rustling sound close by. She turned toward it, seeing something out of the corner of her eye that disappeared before she could actually see it. It made her shiver. She paused, trying to be still, trying to slow her racing heart.

She heard it again and swiveled in its direction, then back to the other side when she heard it there. Suddenly, it was behind her. She spun around, losing her footing at the edge of the hollow-like depression in the earth. She slipped, and as she tried to get her footing, one leg was sucked into the earth.

She fell back, yanking her leg out of the hole, hearing the sound of stones and earth falling, colliding with something, and then plunging into water far below.

Charlotte scrambled back from the edge, panting for breath, when she felt eyes on her. She looked up to see the inscrutable face of the barn owl watching her from the other side of the small crater. It sat perched on one of the stones, watching her with dark obsidian eyes, bits of coal on his snowy face.

"A-are you—" she began, but the bird took flight, heading straight for her. She scrambled back, just managing to get to her feet as the owl swooped toward her, talons outstretched.

She ducked down, putting her arms up to protect her head. She felt a stinging pain in her arm as the bird cried out. It was like it was trying to pull her with it. She pushed against it, and it let go, hovering in mid-air expectantly, its large wings flapping unnaturally slowly in the air.

An overwhelming feeling of panic rose up inside her, and all she could do then was run—and run she did. She ran so fast she barely paid attention to where she was going. Low branches whipped her as she raced through the woods, not caring as they snagged and tore at her coat. She twisted and ran until her coat got caught in the low-hanging branches of a cockspur tree. The owl shrieked behind her, and she desperately tried to yank herself free, but the more she fought the more entangled she became.

Finally, she unzipped her coat and slipped out of it, leaving it torn and dangling from the branch. She barely felt the cold as she ran and ran until she burst through the edge of the woods and out into the open. She didn't stop running for another hundred yards. When she did, her breath was ragged and painful as she gulped down near-freezing air into her lungs.

She scanned the edge of the forest warily, looking for the owl, but saw no sign of him and then suddenly realized her arm didn't hurt anymore. She looked down at it, expecting at least to see a torn shirtsleeve, but her shirt wasn't torn and there was no blood.

Quickly, she shoved her sleeve up, but there weren't even any marks on her skin.

Nothing there, she told herself, looking back at the woods as she slowed her racing heart. *Nothing there.*

With one last deep and still tremulous breath, she started back to Grey Hall as what was left of the sun began to slide beneath a gray and leaden horizon.

CHAPTER EIGHT

CHARLOTTE BARELY ATE ANYTHING at dinner. She pushed the food around her plate, trying to make it look like she'd eaten more than she had, but her parents were on to her.

"Are you feeling all right?" her father asked.

"I'm fine," she said, spearing a piece of broccoli with her fork and forcing it down.

Her mother came around to her side of the table to put a hand to her forehead. "No fever."

"I told you, I'm fine," she protested, hating how whiny she sounded.

"Maybe you should go to bed early. Big day tomorrow. Christmas Eve," her mother said with a hopeful smile.

Charlotte did her best to mimic it. "Right. I am kind of tired. Don't want to miss anything."

After dinner, she quickly made her goodnights and trudged upstairs. She was still unsettled by what had happened that afternoon. How was she ever going to save her father if she couldn't even go into the Dark Woods?

She flopped down onto her bed. She had barely more than one day to find the answers, and she wasn't sure she was any closer than she was when she'd started out.

Helplessness and fear welled up inside, threatening to spill out in tears.

"Did you go into the Dark Woods?" a voice boomed beside her suddenly.

She started, sitting up suddenly to see Phineas looking like a thundercloud at her bedside.

"I . . . I—"

He didn't let her finish and continued to bellow, pacing the short length of her bed as he did. "Have you lost your mind, child? Did I not instruct you, under no circumstances, to go into the woods?"

"I—"

"Did you listen to me? No. Just a ghost, what does it matter what he thinks? He's only been around for *three hundred years!*" The last was said so loudly, she was sure the building would have shaken if it could.

It was too much. It was all just too much. Her fear, her failure, his wrath. It filled her to the point of breaking, and the tears she'd held at bay tumbled down her cheeks.

When a soft sob escaped her lips, Phineas halted his furious pacing and turned to look at her. He tried to glare at her, but his expression faltered and then quickly softened into uncomfortable concern.

"Now, there's—there's no reason for that," he said sharply and then added more gently, "Dry your tears, child."

She wiped at her face with the back of her hand. "I'm sorry. I don't know how I'm going to help my dad. Or you."

He looked almost physically pained by her words. "Hush now. You do yourself a disservice. You are a Cross, are you not?"

She sniffled but straightened as she nodded.

"Of course you are."

"But how can I break the curse if I can't even face the witch?"

Phineas, like her father, always seemed to have the answers, but he looked as helpless as she felt. "I do not know," he confessed.

She'd gathered herself now, her outburst of emotion fading and replaced by purpose again. "You must know more about the curse. Something."

He sighed heavily, looking out of her bedroom window. "I know very little, and I do not see how what I do know will help us."

"What is it?" she asked anxiously, shifting to kneel on the bed. "What do you know?"

"'Upon the day of the coming of the son when, with pure heart, three gifts shalt beest given, peace wilt returneth to Grey Hall,'" he recited before turning back to her.

"Do not ask me what it means for I do not know. I have lived in ignorance as to the meaning of those words for centuries, and I do not expect that to change now."

Charlotte got off the bed. She liked to move around when she was thinking, and she began pacing along the other side of the bed. "Let's take it bit by bit. 'Upon the day of the coming of the son.' Is that S-O-N or S-U-N?"

He paused, looking surprised by the question. "I do not know. I never saw it writ down. I have only heard it spoken."

"It's like Shakespeare," she said, warming to the task, her brain having something other to do than worry. "That part of that play." Phineas looked at her flatly. "You know, um, 'Now is the winter of our discontent—'"

"'Made glorious summer by this son of York,'" he finished for her.

"It's a play on words."

"You are familiar with the Bard?" he asked surprised.

"Some," she admitted, not telling him it was mostly from movies. "But I know that bit. It meant both sun like the one in the sky and son, S-O-N."

"Yes," Phineas said, lost in his own thoughts.

"Maybe it means both. Like sunrise and Christmas Day!" she said excitedly. "The coming of the Son."

"The Son of God? Possibly."

"Okay, so it could mean either or both." She chewed on her lower lip. "And the gifts. Three gifts. Like the Wise Men," she wondered aloud.

"I somehow doubt frankincense and myrrh will solve our problem," he remarked. "Gold possibly."

"You can't count anything out," she said. He didn't look very convinced, and, honestly, neither was she, but it was something.

"Mordecai's wife *was* quite devout," Phineas said thoughtfully. "He, unfortunately, chose to twist religion to his own dark end."

"I read about her, Sarah, in that *History of Grey Hall.* She died in a fire, didn't she?"

"Yes, that was when he built Grey Hall."

Charlotte shuddered to think that the ruins she'd so often played in were and all that was left of the house that had burned down. Pushing that thought aside she asked, "What else?"

"That is all, I fear, save for something a nanny of mine—"

She grinned. "You had a nanny?"

He glowered at her, but the effect had long since worn off. "Yes, as a child. I was a curious sort until I grew out of it and into my responsibilities," he added meaningfully.

"What did she say?"

"When I asked about what had happened—there were rumors even then—all she would say was that the answer lies above his heart." Then he shrugged, an ill-fitting mannerism for a man, or ghost, like Phineas.

"The answer lies above his heart," she repeated. "Whose heart? Mordecai?"

"One can only surmise," he said. "However, I do not see how it is of any help to us. The man clearly had no heart."

"Everyone does," she said more to herself than to Phineas. "His heart . . . Maybe there's a clue on his gravestone?"

"As dull and uninspired as he was, I am afraid it is a simple marker, a rather spartan, unadorned stone befitting the man beneath it."

"Well, it's got to mean something." *It has to.* "Was there anything else? Anything at all?"

"I am afraid not. I tried to warn you that this would serve no purpose."

She frowned, but she wasn't ready to give up yet. Not by a long shot. "Upon the day of the coming of the son when, with pure heart, three gifts shalt beest given, peace wilt returneth to Grey Hall," she recited.

All Phineas could do was nod thoughtfully. Then he looked at her with that same gentle worry her father so often did. "You are certain that you are unharmed after your . . . adventure into the woods?"

Without thinking about it, she rubbed her arm and nodded.

"You must be careful. I do desire to be free of this prison, but not at any price."

She understood what he meant and didn't argue, though there was no price she wasn't willing to pay to save her father.

"Sleep," he said. "Perhaps the answers will come to us with the dawn."

She nodded then started to lay out her pajamas. Despite everything she'd been through that day and the fear that still clutched her heart, she felt better now.

"Thank you," she said, turning back toward him. "I—" But he was gone.

ELIZABETH ROLLED ONTO HER side, half-asleep, an arm reaching out to lie on Simon's chest. She could tell that he was awake by the way his hand covered hers and held it briefly before relaxing. The knowledge pulled her the rest of the way from sleep herself.

She blinked in the darkness, seeing his face outlined against the light from the window as he stared up at the ceiling. He'd probably been doing that all night.

"What time is it?" she mumbled, lifting her head to squint toward the bedside table.

His voice was a soft, deep rumble. "Late. Go back to sleep." Gently, he pressed down on her hand.

She grumbled sleepily, forcing her eyes open. "Simon."

He turned his head to look at her. Even in the dim light, she could see his worry.

"Go back to sleep, darling," he said.

She snuggled in closer. "I will if you will."

He gave a soft laugh that she felt more than heard. "I'm fine. Sleep."

"She's all right."

He gave a half-grunt, half-sigh.

Elizabeth pushed herself up onto her elbow. "She's almost a teenager. She's going to be moody. Honestly, this is probably the calm before the storm."

"Comforting."

It was Elizabeth's turn to laugh.

"Something is bothering her," he said. "And I don't like not knowing what it is."

Elizabeth sighed before settling into his side. "I know. I don't like it either, but I think she just needs a little space. She'll come to us when she's ready."

Simon grumbled discontentedly again.

"You know that if it was something serious," Elizabeth said, "she would tell us."

"Yes," he agreed grudgingly. "I suppose so. But it's not like her to be off her feed." He glanced at his wife. "She comes by that honestly."

Elizabeth nudged him playfully.

He looked back up at the ceiling. "And I think she's not sleeping well."

"She comes by *that* honestly," Elizabeth replied.

He chuckled. "Touché."

Elizabeth slid her hand from beneath his and began to trace idle patterns on his chest. "There are better ways to spend sleepless nights."

He turned his head again, leaning back slightly to get a better look at her. "Are there?"

She smiled slyly, sure he could see it even in the dark.

"It is almost Christmas," she said. "Maybe you could unwrap one of your gifts early."

He captured her wandering hand with his and then pushed himself up, resting his head in one hand. "Did you have one in particular in mind?"

She only nodded, her eyes never leaving his.

He leaned down and kissed her tenderly as his hand cupped her cheek before brushing his fingers lightly down her neck and setting to work on the top button of her pajama top.

She sighed beneath him. "I actually bought some lingerie for this."

"Something to look forward to," he murmured as his lips followed the path his hand had traveled moments before.

"I could put it on," she offered.

"Don't you dare," he said between kisses.

She sighed happily.

"I do love unwrapping a beautiful package," he said, his breath warm against her skin, "but it's what's inside that I adore."

Flushed with both passion and love, she pulled him up for a kiss, and everything else was forgotten.

CHAPTER NINE

IT WAS CHRISTMAS EVE. Charlotte could barely eat anything that morning; her stomach was too busy being tied up in knots. She'd barely slept last night, her mind racing with thoughts of the curse, and how quickly time for her to solve the riddle was running out.

She'd been lucky that her parents had a last-minute errand to run in town or she wasn't sure what she would have done. She needed to get out of the house and think. Her mother had cautioned her to wear her heavy coat—the one currently hanging from a bramble somewhere in the Dark Woods—if she went out. Instead, she pulled on an extra sweater and walked out into the garden. A light snow had started to fall.

She half expected to see the owl there again and wasn't sure if it was a good thing or a bad thing that it wasn't there. When it had flown toward her, she'd panicked. It seemed like the logical reaction at the time, but she wished she hadn't. What had it been trying to do? It felt like it was trying to pull her forward. Bring her to the witch? That hollow? The stones? Was that the holy well Fiona had mentioned? They used to drown witches. The well!

The speed of her thoughts spurred her legs to keep pace. She walked out of the garden and onto the expansive lawn beyond. The witch wanted her to come. To bring the gifts?

"If only I knew what gifts," she muttered to herself.

In the distance, the ruins from the original house loomed larger than they ever had before. It felt almost sacrilegious to go there, knowing what she did now, but she started for them anyway.

There wasn't much left of the house that had once stood there, just a few crumbling stone walls and the fireplace. She walked inside what she'd imagined was the great hall and found her way toward the old fireplace.

She tried to picture the room as it had once been, building walls in her mind where only distant trees stood now, a floor where dirt and bits of frozen snow lay, a warming fire making the room glow.

She stood in front of the fireplace, what there was of it. There was a chimney and mantel with some sort of carving on the façade above the firebox with the large hearth below.

She started to turn away, but a thought came to her.

The hearth. His hearth. His heart?

"'The answer lies above his heart,'" she recited. "Hearth?"

She stared up at the stone carving above the mantel, her heart starting to race, but it was so dirty after hundreds of years of neglect she couldn't make much of it out.

Finding a fallen branch with a few leaves still attached, she used it as a broom, trying to brush away some of the grime. It didn't do much good. She needed to get a ladder and cleaning supplies!

She raced back into the house, bursting into the kitchen. Mrs. Carter yelped in surprise.

"Sorry!" Charlotte said, skidding to a halt. "Cleaning stuff? Brush, sponge, everything!"

Mrs. Carter regained her composure and looked at Charlotte with narrowed eyes. "And why would you be needing that?"

"It's . . . it's a Christmas surprise," Charlotte said, praying that would be answer enough. Thankfully, it was.

Mrs. Carter looked suspicious but gestured to a small closet. Charlotte dashed forward and started grabbing everything she'd need.

"I expect all of that to be put back where it belongs when you're finished," Mrs. Carter said.

Charlotte tossed a promise over her shoulder and ran back outside. After she dumped her supplies, she found a step ladder in one of the sheds. It took her nearly half an hour to clean off enough gunk to bring the carving to life again.

Hands wet and cold, she stepped back to get a better view. It looked a little like a coat of arms, but it wasn't one she was familiar with. Above the sort of shield-like part where a crest would usually go, there were two hands cupped together. Beneath that, the shield part was divided into three sections. The upper left was a chalice of some kind. Next to it in the upper right was a vaguely familiar type of flower with little star-shaped petals covering most of the stem. Beneath that, in the third area, was a heart.

She stared at it thoughtfully. The hands at the top—they looked like they were offering something. Three sections—three gifts. This had to be it! A cup, a flower, and a heart?

The elation she'd felt at having found the clue quickly began to fade. What did it mean? What sort of cup? A cup of tea? A bouquet of flowers? And a heart? Hoping it wasn't the eye of newt kind of heart, she shuddered.

No, it wouldn't be. It was something else. They all meant something else.

But what?

THAT EVENING WAS IMPOSSIBLY long. Her parents seemed pleased with themselves. Whatever errand they'd run in town had made them happy. She'd asked them what it was. They said it was a secret and that she'd find out tomorrow.

Charlotte went through the motions, trying her best to pretend the end of the world—the end of *her* world—wasn't just hours away. They had a special Christmas Eve dinner, watched *White Christmas*, had hot chocolate, and opened one present each. When they'd called Jack she'd done her best to sound like her usual self, but even over the phone he seemed to sense something was wrong. How she wished she could have told him everything.

She put on a smile and endured Christmas Eve, but all she could think about was tomorrow.

Christmas Day.

Upon the day of the coming of the son . . . Did that mean she only had until sunrise tomorrow to figure it out? And if she didn't . . . Tears welled in her eyes, but she scrubbed them away with a defiant swipe of her hands.

"I'm not giving up."

"I would expect no less," Phineas said, appearing at the foot of her bed.

"Oh, Phineas," she said, feeling the weight of it all, "I don't know what to do."

He took a halting half-step toward her before stopping, his outstretched hand falling to his side. "I know, child."

"I found a clue, I think. There's a carving above the hearth in the old house."

After she'd told him about what she'd found, he murmured, "So close and yet so far."

There was a knock on the door, and her dad poked her head inside. "Just checking in. You all right?"

Charlotte nodded, not trusting her voice not to betray her.

"Darling, you know you can tell us anything," he said, coming to stand just inside the door. "We're always here for you."

If only she could!

The tears she'd almost kept at bay filled her eyes, and she flew off the bed and ran toward, colliding so hard against him that she heard his "*oof.*"

"What's going on, sweetheart?" he lamented as he held her.

She shook her head and then pressed it against his chest, holding him as tightly as she could.

After a few moments, he eased her back. "Tell me what's wrong? Please."

She shook her head, forcing a smile to her face, and he gently touched her cheek.

"Charlotte."

"I love you, Dad," she said and hugged him tightly again.

She could feel him caressing her hair before he leaned down to press a kiss to the top of her head. "I love you too, darling."

Oh, how she wanted to tell him everything. He would know what to do. He was so much smarter than she was. He would have been able to solve the puzzle already.

"Get some rest, sweetheart," he said, easing her back. "And if you need us, we're just down the hall."

She nodded bravely as he turned to leave.

"Dad."

He paused, but whatever she was going to say stuck in her throat. She shook her head. He gave a comforting but concerned smile and left.

Once the door had closed, she fell back onto her bed and cried until she ran out of tears.

It was very late that night when Ambrose stuck his head through the door to her room, one hand covering his eyes. "Are you decent?"

Despite everything she laughed. "You can come in, Ambrose."

"I heard you moving about." He dropped his hand, grinned at her, and strode through the doorway. "Phineas told me you found a clue. I knew you were smart."

"Not smart enough," she said. She'd been thinking about it for hours and hours and wasn't any closer to figuring out what she was supposed to do. She'd been so focused on the solution to the curse she hadn't even changed into her pajamas.

"Maybe you need to take your mind off things? Of course, my mother always said I never put mine *to* anything."

She giggled.

"I could do cartwheels to entertain you. I used to be able to juggle, but now . . ." He tried to pick up a small figurine up from a shelf, but his hand just passed right through it.

"I always thought ghosts rattled chains and made things go bump in the night," she said.

"Oh, yes. Some do. Unpleasant ghosts." He leaned in close, raising a conspiratorial hand to the side of his mouth. "They have issues."

She couldn't help but laugh again. "You're all so different than I thought. At first, I thought Phineas was mean, but he's not. Not really."

"Sometimes, things are not as they seem."

She nodded, and then a thought flitted across her mind. *Not as they seem.*

She sprang off her bed and fumbled around on her desk for a pad and pencil. "You said before that you were good with flowers."

"A green thumb and two left feet."

Quickly, she sketched out the flowers from the carving above Mordecai's hearth and held it up for him to see. It wasn't perfect, but it was close enough. "What flowers are these?"

He squinted at it and then drew back. "Hyacinth," he announced.

"Hyacinth. You're sure?"

He made a face. "I am not good for many things, but I do know my flowers. That is hyacinth, but I am afraid it won't help you much. It blooms in the spring. There is none to be found at this time of year."

"That's okay," she said, a broad smile coming to her face and hope lifting her heart. "It's not what it seems."

CHAPTER TEN

CHARLOTTE PULLED OPEN THE door to the library. "It's not about flowers at all," she said in a hushed but excited voice.

Ambrose followed her inside. "I do not understand."

Turning on the light, she strode over to the bookcase and began purposefully scanning the shelves. "Flowers have meanings. It's why you give someone you love red roses and yellow for friendship. They all mean *something*. They have a language all their own."

He looked at her as if she'd just pulled down the moon and held it in her hands. "Yes," he breathed. "Yes!"

She hurriedly skimmed over the titles until she found the one she was looking for—*The Language of Flowers: Their Meanings and Devotions.* Her fingers almost trembled with anticipation as she turned through the pages.

"Hyacinth," she read out loud, "symbolizes forgiveness." She looked at Ambrose, her eyes bright with possibilities now. "Forgiveness. That's one of the gifts!"

"Oh!" Ambrose said clasping his hands excitedly. "What of the others?"

"I . . . I don't know," she said, silently adding a very certain "yet" afterward. "There was a cup and a heart. The heart probably means love, but . . . am I supposed to love the witch?" she asked doubtfully.

Ambrose frowned at the idea.

"And the cup?" She sat down heavily in one of the reading chairs, the book forgotten now. "What does that mean?"

"She needs a drink?" Ambrose offered tentatively, earning a scowl in miniature from Charlotte.

"It wasn't exactly a cup; it was fancier, like a chalice."

"She wants a nice drink?"

"Ambrose."

"I'm sorry. I'm not very good at this sort of thing."

"Without you I wouldn't have known that the flower was hyacinth. You've already been a big help."

His ample chest puffed out at the compliment as he beamed back at her.

"A cup, a chalice," she muttered to herself. "What do they mean?"

"Well," Ambrose began cautiously.

"Don't say it means to give her a drink," Charlotte cut him off, but then stopped. "Or maybe it does. Giving water to the thirsty. It's mercy! It's an act of mercy. That's got to be it! An act of forgiveness. An act of mercy. And an act of love!"

"Do you think so?" Ambrose asked nearly breathless with anticipation.

"Yes. That's got to be it."

The grandfather clock down the hall chimed three. Sunrise was in just a few hours. Time was running out.

Suddenly, she started for the door.

"Where are you going?" Ambrose asked worriedly.

"To see the witch."

"It's the middle of the night," he protested.

"I know, but I don't have a choice. It'll be light in just a few hours and . . ." She couldn't even finish that thought.

Ambrose hurried to stand in front of the door, planting his feet and placing his hands on his hips. "I cannot allow you to go."

She stepped right through him and opened the door.

"Oh dear," he groaned as she strode down the hallway. "Charlotte!"

He chased after her down the hall. "You mustn't go alone."

"I don't have any choice," she said. "I can't tell my parents. I've tried."

She took her coat from the closet. It wasn't nearly warm enough for this, but it would have to do. At the last minute, she grabbed a small flashlight as well.

"What's going on here?" Phineas demanded as he appeared at their side. Nicky slid through the wall behind him, casually plucking at a piece of lint on his jacket.

"She's going to see the witch again!" Ambrose said.

"You most certainly are not," Phineas declared.

"I have to. I know what to do now." She buttoned up her coat and headed for the back door.

"It is far too dangerous," he said.

Her courage faltered briefly, but she took a deep breath. She wasn't going to let something happen to her father if she could help it.

"Please, child," Phineas asked, that softness back in his voice.

"I have to," she told him.

He straightened, looking very much like he did in his portrait. "I forbid it."

She eyed him suspiciously. "Can you do that?"

"I have already done it, have I not?"

She reached for the door, half expecting the knob not to turn in her hand, but it did, and she pulled the door open, letting in a burst of cold air.

"Charlotte," Phineas pleaded.

"She knows what she's about," Nicky said. "Trust her."

"She is a child," Phineas barked at him.

"She is a Cross," Nicky replied.

Phineas looked at her with a mixture of anger and regret. "Would that I could take your place," he said. "Or at least accompany you, but we are trapped within the walls of this blasted house!"

"It'll be okay," Charlotte told him. "I know what I have to do. What I have to give her."

"Oh, child," he said softly, as she hurried out the door, "do you?"

At least it had stopped snowing, she thought as she shivered against the cold wind. It was dark, but the moon was full, and there were only a few clouds in the sky. She stuffed her hands into her coat pockets, wishing she'd taken the time to get her scarf and gloves, but there was nothing to be done about it now. There wasn't time to go back home, and if she did, she wasn't sure she'd have the courage to leave it again.

She looked across the silent field of freshly fallen snow. The world after a snow was always so quiet. As she walked on toward the Dark Woods, all she could hear were her own footsteps and the sound of her breath and the beat of her heart.

I won't let you down. Any of you. I won't.

THE THREE GHOSTS STOOD at the threshold watching Charlotte disappear into the darkness.

"Are you really going to let her go?" Ambrose asked.

"What would you have me do?" Phineas barked at him. He glared at him and then turned back to watch the night one last time. "I need a drink," he muttered, before barking out, "Blasted curse!"

He stormed off, walking through tables and walls on his way to the library, Nicky and Ambrose following along in his wake.

He strode into the library, hating how quiet it was now. He'd so often loathed the unceasing cacophony most people made, centuries of terrible music, endless chatter, and that godforsaken television. But now, the house was too still. Too quiet. It would not do.

Restlessly, he stalked across the room until he came to the book of flowers, the girl's sketch of the hyacinth resting upon it.

He should have found a way to stop her. He was losing his touch. No man or woman had ever failed to quail under his gaze before. This child was impossible.

The gifts—they would not be given easily, that he knew. The child had no idea the price she would be asked to pay. No curse that had killed and tortured for hundreds of years would be easily broken. The witch would demand like for like, of that he was sure. His freedom for her . . .

"No," he whispered.

It could not be. He would not let it be. "This must not be."

There had to be some way to stop her.

"What can we do?" Ambrose asked plaintively.

"Her parents. They must be informed of what is happening. They are the only ones who can stop her now."

"But how?" Ambrose cried. "We cannot reach them."

Phineas began to pace and a memory flashed through the torrent in his mind. "Perhaps we can," he said, pausing. "He . . . sensed our presence, did he not?"

"He did!" Ambrose said excitedly.

"You should trust the girl," Nicky said as he flopped into a chair.

Phineas barely spared him glare before returning to his mind to the task. "Perhaps we can communicate with them."

"Through a series of chills and shivers?" Nicky added, miming both.

Phineas's scowl deepened. "There must be a way."

"I could pull a book off the shelf," Ambrose said. "You remember that I did that once."

"Yes," Nicky said, stretching out his long legs in front of him. "And you were nearly insensate for a week from the effort." He sat up straight suddenly, a grin on his face. "Do it again."

Ignoring Nicholas, Phineas stroked his beard. "It can be done. It does require great effort, but an object can be moved."

"I'm sure un-shelving a book will explain everything," Nicky said, slouching indolently again.

"If we can awaken them and draw them to her room . . ." Phineas ventured.

"Yes. They will see she is missing and go to save her."

"And what of her father?" Nicky asked. "You condemn him to death?"

"You were a father—appalling as that is," Phineas ground out. "Would you want your child to die in your place?"

Nicky sat up again, all humor gone. "Die?"

"What do you think the price will be? A basket full of kittens?"

"I . . . I didn't think."

"As usual," Phineas said. "We must find a way to warn them. We must."

THE DARK WOODS LOOKED impossibly dark. They'd been difficult enough to navigate during the day; at night, it was doubly imposing. As she neared the edge of the pasture, she turned on her little flashlight. The moon was enough to see by out in the open, but in the woods . . .

The little beam of light cut through the darkness and then faded, swallowed by the night. The canopy of trees blocked almost all of the ambient light. Taking a bracing breath, she stepped forward into the blackness.

The snow here was icy and crunched beneath her boots. Her breath was like billowing steam, lasting for a fleeting moment and then disappearing. She hunched her shoulders to try to keep warm, but the cold she felt had little to do with the temperature.

Be brave, she told herself. That's what her parents would do. They would be brave.

The thought of them spurred her on, and she walked deeper into the woods. It was painfully quiet now, and the sound of her footsteps in the cracking snow echoed amongst the dark and shadowy trees. Suddenly, she heard something to her right and stopped, shining her light that way. But the small flashlight could only illuminate so far before the black night stopped it like a wall. It was almost worse being able to see just a little, knowing that anything could be just out of sight. Almost worse.

A cry came from behind her, and she spun around. Her heart raced in her chest until she realized it was just a fox in the distance. It was such a painful, lonely cry. Twice more it sounded before the forest fell into an unnatural silence again.

She pressed on, her heart lodged firmly in her throat now. She tried to swallow it down, but it wouldn't budge. Carefully, step by step, she moved deeper and deeper into the forest.

After another ten minutes, she thought she had to be close. The little hollow couldn't be too far away now. Then she saw the owl, perched silently on a low-hanging branch. It watched her with those inscrutable eyes.

"I've come to see your mistress," she told it. "Elara Prynce."

The owl shrieked once in what she took as acknowledgment, and Charlotte walked toward it.

"Am I going the right way?" she asked it.

It simply stared at her, its white oval face standing out in the sea of darkness.

"Some help you are," she muttered and pressed on.

The owl cried once more and took off, flying past her. She shifted her course and followed.

A few minutes later, they reached the edge of the little hollow. The owl perched on the far side of it, just as it had before. It watched her and then cried, stretching its wings.

"Hello?" she called out. When no answer came, she tried again. "Hello?!"

The owl cried once more and flapped its wings, seeming to beckon her forward.

Fear nearly kept her still, but she wasn't going to let anything happen to her father. She wasn't. Cautiously, Charlotte took a step forward and then another.

She took one more step, but suddenly, there was nothing to hold her. Her foot sank below the mossy ground, and bits of earth fell away as a giant hole opened up beneath her. She tried to turn back, to reach back to grab on to something, anything, but it was no use. The ground fell away beneath her, and she plunged into darkness.

CHAPTER ELEVEN

Phineas stood in the hallway outside the master bedchamber. "Are you ready?"

Nicky, who was halfway down the hall, gave him a jaunty little salute, while Ambrose took up his position outside of Charlotte's bedroom and whispered something Phineas couldn't make out.

"Speak up, man!" Phineas bellowed. "They can't hear you."

"Not to mention that we're *trying* to wake them," Nicky added. "Hellooo?"

"I am ready," Ambrose called out, still in a hoarse whisper.

"I am surrounded by fools and jackanapes," Phineas muttered to himself. He glared at them as best he could from such a distance. "When it is your turn—do your part."

With that, he walked through the door of the master suite and over to the large bed, eying the sleeping couple thoughtfully.

"This would so much easier if you could hear me. I don't suppose . . ." He leaned down close to Simon's ear. "Wake up!" he roared.

Nothing.

With a sigh, he stood and looked for something to move. Thankfully, a large tome sat on the bedside table. *In Search of Lost Time.*

"Curious," Phineas whispered intrigued, but his interest would have to wait.

As a ghost and not a poltergeist, his form was relegated to the spirit world, only able to interact with the material plane with great effort. Where poltergeists were trapped between the worlds, he was merely a phantom to the living. To move a corporeal object as a non-corporeal entity required intense concentration.

He focused on the book, directing all his energy toward it. He could feel the barrier, the veil between worlds, keeping him from his goal. He would not be denied, though, and pushed through the wall between that which was and that which is. The book began to move, shuddering slightly, before it started to inch its way toward the edge of the table.

Had he a body, it would have been trembling from the effort. As it was, he felt every ounce of his being reaching, pushing. With one final burst of will, he commanded the book to move.

With a loud *thump*, it hit the floor, and he turned his attention back to the occupants of the bed.

Simon sat up with a start, but the woman merely groaned and rolled over. Was she unwell?

It took Simon a moment to notice the book. "What the . . .?"

"Now, Nicholas!" Phineas yelled.

A few agonizing moments later, there was a crash out in the hall.

Simon touched his wife's shoulder. "Elizabeth. Wake up."

The woman lifted her head but kept her eyes closed. "Is it present time?"

"Wake up," Simon repeated as he swiveled out of bed.

"What is it?" Elizabeth finally sat up, scrubbing her eyes.

"I don't know." Simon picked up her robe from the end of the bed, tossing it in her direction, before slipping on his own. "I heard something out in the hall."

Cautiously, they made their way to the door. Simon opened it and peered into the hallway. Phineas tagged along, joining Nicholas in the hall. Save for the two ghosts, the corridor was empty, dimly lit by the half-flames of a wall sconce.

Simon and Elizabeth walked slowly down the hall, stopping when they came to a large, and very expensive vase, or what had been a large and very expensive vase but was now no more than shards upon the floor.

"What's going on?" Elizabeth asked warily.

"I don't know," Simon said as he stepped around the broken pieces, careful to keep his wife shielded and behind him as they walked on.

When they drew near enough, Phineas called out, "Now, Ambrose!"

There was an interminable wait as the couple walked down the hall, paused, and turned back the other way. If they went too far they wouldn't be drawn to the child's room.

"Ambrose!" Phineas cried urgently.

Finally, there was a crash from inside the girl's room. Her parents stopped mid-step. Phineas could tell from the looks in their eyes that they realized where the sound had come from.

"Charlotte!" Simon called out as they both ran toward their daughter's bedroom.

Simon yanked open the door, racing inside.

A lamp lay on its side, the glass dome lying broken on the floor.

"Simon," Elizabeth breathed. She stood next to the bed—the empty bed. "She's not here."

"What in the . . . Charlotte!"

Phineas felt a wave of triumph, but it was tempered by the fact that they'd not yet realized where the child was.

Searching for her, they opened the door to the closet and even the wardrobe before moving back out into the hall, all three ghosts following along behind.

"She's probably in the library," Simon told his wife reassuringly.

She was not. Nor was she in the kitchens or the gallery or the salon. Finally, they woke the Carters, but neither had seen the girl since early last night.

"Where the hell is she?" Simon demanded to the empty hall.

Elizabeth shuddered. "Do you feel that?"

Simon nodded. "Cold air." They both headed in the direction of the chilling breeze. The backdoor near the kitchen was open. In her haste, the child hadn't closed it properly.

Thank heaven for small favors, Phineas thought.

"She wouldn't go out. Not in the middle of the night," Simon said.

Elizabeth hurried to the closet, pulling the door open and rifling through the contents. "Her coat's gone."

"Bloody hell."

IT FELT LIKE THE earth was swallowing her whole, and Charlotte screamed as she fell. The world flew by in a cloud of sod and dirt and rocks until it all stopped—suddenly and painfully. She landed with a thud that knocked the wind out of her. She winced in pain and gasped for air as dirt and debris rained down from above, splashing into the shallow puddles at the bottom of the hole.

Finally getting her breath, she looked up at the hole above her, squinting as dirt fell into her eyes. The starry sky was just visible through the open wound in the earth overhead. She coughed, waving her hand to brush away the dirt, wincing a bit as she did.

A chill overtook her as she realized she'd landed in a shallow puddle of water; it was enough to soak her jeans and jacket sleeve.

Her arm hurt from her awkward landing but not too badly. She gathered herself and then crawled around on the ground trying to find the flashlight she'd dropped when she fell. Her hand landed on the cold metal handle, and she tried the switch. Nothing. She hit it a few times with the heel of her hand, and the light, weak and flickering, came back to life. The beam of light landed on something white. She stepped forward and then drew back quickly, her foot slipping on a wet rock, as she realized what it was—a skeleton.

The clothes it had once worn were barely scraps of fraying cloth now, but a large pendant still hung around its neck. As if compelled, she reached out for it but stopped when a woman's voice came from behind her.

"Do not touch that."

CHAPTER TWELVE

"**T**HIS WAY!" SIMON CALLED out.

Once they'd discovered Charlotte was missing, they'd hurriedly dressed, grabbed flashlights, and headed out the back door to search for her.

What on earth was she thinking?

Elizabeth tried to control her anger. Anger at her daughter for running off in the middle of the night, and in the middle of winter! But mostly anger at herself for not having taken more seriously the warning signs that something was wrong. Simon had, but she'd written Charlotte's behavior off as pre-teen drama. And now . . .

She shivered at the thought and then buried it as she ran to where Simon was standing just outside of the side garden gate.

"Thank God for fresh snow," he said as Elizabeth came to his side.

Her little footprints were visible in clear a line leading off across the snow.

They set off after her, Simon not regulating his long stride as he normally did, and Elizabeth had to half-jog to keep up the pace he set.

She knew from the set of his jaw that he was angry too, at Charlotte and at her.

"I'm sorry," she said, the cold already biting her cheeks. "You were right. There was something else going on. I should have listened to you."

"We can worry about that later," he said.

But Elizabeth was worried about that now, and about Charlotte. What was going on with her? How could it be so serious that she'd run off in the middle of the night? How hadn't they known?

It was as if every confidence she had in her ability as a parent had been stripped away in one fell swoop. She started to question everything, every decision she'd made, every moment they'd spent together since arriving here.

Charlotte had been her usual self before they'd come to Grey Hall. What had happened to upset her had happened here. Not knowing what was eating Elizabeth alive.

"I'll never forgive myself," she said, more to herself than to Simon.

"Don't," he said tersely. "We'll find her."

Elizabeth had to believe it or she'd lose her mind.

"Where is she going?" Elizabeth asked as they followed the footprints across the sloping lawn to the large field beyond. In the distance, the inky black of the forest rose up from the white of the snow.

"I think I have an idea," he muttered.

"Why would she go into the Dark Woods?" Elizabeth asked. "Why now?"

For that, Simon had no answer.

CHARLOTTE FELT A CHILL at the sound of the voice behind her and slowly turned around to face the witch. The woman wasn't vaguely transparent like Phineas and the others were. She looked solid, real, and very angry.

"Who are you?" the woman demanded.

"I . . ." Charlotte faltered and swallowed.

Elara Prynce wasn't what she'd envisioned. She'd pictured, much to her shame, an old hag like the sort in fairy tales, but the woman standing in front of her wasn't old, not really. She looked to be a little older than her mom maybe, with striking pale eyes and long, dark hair with a streak of grey. She didn't have giant moles or a hooked nose or long spiky fingers. She looked just like . . . a person, although a bit pinched like she was in pain. She looked like a perfectly normal person, one who was dead and a ghost and had cast a spell that might kill her father.

That thought cemented her wavering courage.

"I'm Charlotte Cross."

The woman's eyes flashed. "Cross?"

"Yes," Charlotte said, drawing herself up to her full height, such as it was, "and you're Elara Prynce."

"How do you know my name?"

"You're the witch of the woods. You put a curse on my family."

Elara grinned darkly. "I did."

Charlotte swallowed and lifted her chin. "I'm here to break it."

Elara looked at her with a crooked smile and then started to laugh, lightly at first but with growing fervor.

"It's not funny!" Charlotte said. Nothing about this was funny.

"You'll forgive me, but I have been alone for so long. I think I've gone a bit mad."

"Were you mad when you killed my ancestors?" Charlotte asked, instantly regretting the outburst.

The witch's expression turned stone-faced. "Your ancestors brought that upon themselves."

"They were innocent," Charlotte countered. "Mordec—"

"Do not speak that name!" the woman roared, and the walls around them seemed to tremble at the ferocity of it.

They were walls, Charlotte belatedly realized. And the water. She'd fallen into the well.

From above, the owl shrieked and flew down, circling and calling out, until the witch held out her arm for it to land upon.

"I am sorry, Taliesin," she told the owl, gently stroking its feathered head. "I did not mean to frighten you."

The kind look she gave the owl vanished when she turned her attention back to Charlotte. She glared at her with fury, but Charlotte thought there was also pain in her eyes.

The owl flew off her arm, landing on the skull of the skeleton.

"Leave me," Elara said with a dismissive wave of her hand. "Begone and tell your stories of the witch of the woods."

"No."

The startlement on the woman's face would have been funny under different circumstances.

"What did you say?" the witch said slowly, biting each word.

Charlotte swallowed and planted her feet, ignoring the little splash that they made. She couldn't, and wouldn't, leave until she'd done all she could possibly do to save her father, and Ambrose and Phineas and Nicky, and maybe even her own grandson, she realized.

"I'm here to break the curse."

It might have been wishful thinking on her part, but Charlotte thought she saw hope flicker briefly in the woman's eyes.

"I . . . I've come to give you three gifts."

Elara watched her now with guarded interest, but that shadow of pain never left her eyes.

"Have you?"

"Y-yes. I've been thinking about them all night."

"All night?" the witch laughed. "All night," she repeated mockingly before taking a threatening step forward. "I have been entombed here for four hundred years!"

"I . . . I know. I'm sorry about that. I am. What Morde—"

Elara's eyes flashed in warning.

"What *he* did," Charlotte went on, "was wrong. You had every right to celebrate Winter Solstice."

"How do you know about that?"

"Your . . . a woman, Fiona, she's your descendent. She told me."

"My descendent?" Elara seemed surprised by the prospect of it.

"She's very nice and pretty."

"What does that matter?" the witch asked caustically.

"It . . . It doesn't. But she is. And what Mor—he did to you was just awful. He drowned you here, didn't he?" She glanced over at the skeleton.

"On Yule," Elara said, clearly lost in the horror of that memory.

"And so you cursed us," Charlotte said. "All of us."

"It was well deserved," she ground out.

"It wasn't," Charlotte insisted, earning a fierce glare from the witch. "It was horrible what happened to you, but my father didn't have anything to do with it!"

"Your father?" Elara asked and then a knowing smile came to her face. "Ah, yes. It is time again, is it not?"

"I'm not going to let you hurt him."

"What's done is done," Elara said, sounding almost tired now.

"What's done can be undone," Charlotte said. "I figured it out."

"Have you, child?" Elara asked, mocking her again.

Charlotte ignored the tone and pushed forward. "Three gifts. First is an act of forgiveness," she said. "I forgive you."

Elara laughed. "You forgive me?"

"Yes," Charlotte said, undaunted. She knew—knew in her very soul—what was needed even if the witch herself didn't. "I know you don't forgive

Mor—him for what he did. But I forgive you for what you did, for casting the curse on my family, for what happened to Phineas and Ambrose and Nicholas."

The woman watched her warily now, a cautious hope lighting her eyes.

"I forgive you," Charlotte said again.

The pendant around the skeleton's neck glowed and then dulled again. The witch gasped and looked at Charlotte with new eyes. "You meant that."

It was as if she simply could not imagine a world where forgiveness could be real.

Charlotte nodded and pressed on, gesturing toward the pendant. "Is that what holds your power?"

"It holds my soul," Elara said in a voice so soft Charlotte almost didn't hear her.

Charlotte knew what she had to do next. She reached for the pendant, but the owl screeched at her and flapped its wings in warning.

"I need to bring that out of the well," Charlotte said. "An act of mercy."

"You would set me free?" Elara asked, her voice tremulous.

Charlotte nodded again, hoping the woman believed her.

Without looking away from Charlotte, Elara said, "Move away, Taliesin."

The owl gave a cry of protest but left its perch.

Carefully, Charlotte removed the pendant. "Your talisman?"

The witch nodded. "Yes."

Charlotte tucked it into her pocket and looked at the walls of the well. The stones were uneven, and it was about fifteen feet up to the top. She could do it though. She had to do it. The light from the hole above was already changing. Dawn was coming.

Her arm hurt as she reached for the first handhold, but she ignored it. Her fingers were nearly numb from the cold and the wet, and she flexed them, rubbing her hands together before starting to climb.

The stones were cold beneath her fingers, and a few were slippery to the touch. She gripped one, pulling herself up, and then found a small foothold. It was a good thing she was little; big feet never would have fit.

She was about eight feet up when the stone she grabbed gave way. It tumbled out of her grip, falling to the floor of the well. She cried out, barely able to hold on with her other hand. One foot slipped as she struggled to keep from falling. Somehow, she managed to get her foot back on the narrow ledge of rock.

Her heart was nearly pounding through her chest. "Oh, that was close."

She took a moment to gather herself and her courage again, puffed out a breath, and reached for the next stone.

"Simon!" Elizabeth called out. The distress in her voice sent an icy chill down his spine.

"What is it?" he asked as he turned toward her, belatedly realizing that she'd stopped a few paces back. Her flashlight shone to the right of the rough path they followed in the woods, and his breath caught at what he saw.

Dangling from a low-hanging branch was Charlotte's coat. They both ran toward it, calling out her name, but she was nowhere to be seen. The coat was damp and torn.

He pulled it from the thorns, crushing the fabric in his hands.

Oh, Charlotte.

She was nearly at the top now. Just a few another two feet or so. The last stone was too far though. She stretched as far as she could, pushing herself up on tiptoes, fingers reaching to grasp the edge of it, but it was just too far away. She looked down and swallowed, and then back up, the light of predawn making the sky above her a steely gray.

Time was running out. She had to find a way.

She tried again, her outstretched fingers just inches away from the last handhold. There was nothing else to grab on to. If she was going to get out, she had to grasp it.

There was nothing left to do but jump . . . and pray.

Taking a deep, calming breath, she focused on the stone and then jumped up to grab it. For a fleeting moment, she was weightless, hanging in the air, and then her fingers clutched at it, wrapping around the smooth edges. She'd done it! But when she had to bear her weight, and her fingers slipped. She clawed at the stone, trying desperately to hold on, but it slid from her grasp, and she started to fall.

The cry from her lips was cut short as a strong hand wrapped itself around her wrist. Breathless, she looked up to see her father's face staring down at her.

"Dad?"

CHAPTER THIRTEEN

"CHARLOTTE!" HER FATHER PULLED her out of the well, setting her on her feet next to her mother.

"What are you doing here?" Charlotte asked.

"Are you hurt?" Simon demanded, running his hands up and down her arms, scanning her for injuries.

She shook her head in answer to his question and asked again. "What are you doing here? You shouldn't be here."

"We shouldn't be here?" Elizabeth said, touching her face gently like she did when she had a fever. "Honey?"

"I'm okay. I . . ." She wasn't sure what to say, how to explain what was happening, and was saved the trouble when suddenly the witch appeared, standing at the edge of the well.

Protectively, Simon pulled Charlotte behind him as Elizabeth stepped back, pulling Charlotte tightly to her side.

"What in the name of—Who are you? What are you?" Simon demanded, hands raised to fend her off.

Elara looked at them curiously before turning her attention back to Charlotte. "You kept your word."

"What word?" Simon asked. "What is going on here? What have you done to our daughter?"

The witch never took her eyes off Charlotte. "We have unfinished business, you and I."

"I don't know what business you've got," Elizabeth said sharply, "but it's not with *our* kid."

The sun was just beginning to rise above the horizon. Time was running out!

"Mom, Dad, you trust me, don't you?" Charlotte said desperately.

"We did before you ran off in the middle of the night," her father said tersely, "and got involved with . . . whatever she is!"

"Please, you've got to trust me. Just for a few minutes. Please?" She was begging now, pleading with them to understand things they couldn't possibly understand. "I'll explain everything, I promise, but there's something I need to do."

"Charlotte, we—" her mother began.

"Please?"

"You're the witch of the woods," Simon said to the woman, a sudden look of realization on his face. "What do you want with my daughter? What have you done to her?"

"I have done nothing," she said calmly. "She came to me."

"Please!" Charlotte begged, tugging on his sleeve. "We're almost out of time. Please trust me! I know I haven't given you any reason to, but I need you to. I've never needed you to trust me more than I do right now. Please!"

Her anguished plea reached them. They looked at the witch and then at each other.

"Oh, please?" Charlotte implored them. There were only minutes left before the curse would strike again, before it would take her father.

It was a humbling sign of trust that her father released his iron grip on her shoulder. Both of her parents were wary and stayed close behind her, but they didn't physically hold her back any longer.

Charlotte took a few steps toward the witch.

"That's close enough," her mother cautioned her.

Charlotte could feel her father just a pace behind her, ready to snatch her out of harm's way if need be.

Charlotte stopped several steps away from the witch and held out the talisman. The witch's eyes lit as if the flames of a fire were reflected in them. She reached out a hand and, without touching it, the talisman was suddenly around her neck.

She closed her eyes with obvious pleasure at having it back and let out a satisfied breath. "Yes."

"Charlotte," Simon said warily.

When the witch opened her eyes they glowed briefly before returning to their normal color. She fixed them on Charlotte. "You have one more gift for me."

Charlotte nodded.

"An act of love," Elara said. "What do you offer me?"

"The only thing I have left to give," Charlotte said, less afraid of this moment than she thought she would be. "Me."

"Charlotte!" her father cried, striding forward only to be met with an invisible wall. "Charlotte!"

He beat against the barrier separating them, her mother at his side, trying to reach their daughter but unable to.

"It's okay," she told them before turning back to Elara, ready for whatever came next.

The steely grey of dawn was giving way to a warm golden. The sun was rising.

Elara narrowed her eyes. "You?"

Charlotte nodded. "For him," she said, gesturing toward her father.

"No!" Simon barked. "Whatever is happening here, I forbid it. Charlotte!"

Elara ignored him, her eyes filled with such disbelief, and such intensity that Charlotte could feel the weight of them. "You would offer yourself in his place?"

"Simon!" Elizabeth screamed as they both tried in vain to get through the invisible barrier.

Charlotte nodded again, her vaunted courage starting to crack at the sound of her parents' despair. "He'll be okay, right? And the others will be free?"

Elara watched her carefully, measuring and weighing her. "You do this freely."

Charlotte didn't trust her voice anymore and could only nod.

The talisman around the witch's neck suddenly glowed with a white light. It spread through her chest and then burst out in a blinding flash of light. The explosion of light pushed out in an ever-broadening circle, sweeping over them and through the trees and beyond.

Charlotte could feel it pass through her, like the concussion wave of a small explosion, but it didn't push against her; it passed through her. From the looks on her parents' faces, they'd felt it too.

Elara seemed to sag a little but then stood tall again. There was something different about her now, and then Charlotte realized what it was. The pain, that pinched look, was gone, and the woman smiled.

She ran her hands down her arms as if feeling them for the first time in far too long and patted her face. "It is gone."

"The curse?" Charlotte asked, holding her breath.

"And the pain," Elara said. "So many years of pain." She looked at Charlotte with startled gratitude.

"But you weren't cursed," Charlotte said, not understanding.

"Oh, but I was in my way. No one can cast such a spell without consequence. Hate and fear wound the person who wields them just as much as those who are their object. In my anger I condemned myself as well." Her eyes lit again with a brightness, light and pure. "But now I am free. Thanks to you, child."

Charlotte swallowed. This was it. "Will you take me away now?"

The witch smiled again and stepped forward, going down to her knees before her. "No, my dear girl. You are safe. You have freed me from the well and from my pain and have broken the curse. I had long ago lost hope that anyone in this world was pure enough of heart to do so, but . . . fear not now. It was never your life that was the bargain, only your true offering of it."

"So, it's over? My dad's safe?"

"Yes, child. He is. It is over." She stood. "Finally over."

She waved her hand, releasing Simon and Elizabeth, who rushed forward to stand protectively on either side of Charlotte.

"I'm sorry," Charlotte told her. "For all of it."

Elara shook her head and offered her a small smile. "It is past now."

She held out her arm and called for her familiar. "Taliesin!" The owl flew out of the well, landing on her hand.

She looked at Charlotte one last time. "*Nollaig shona dhuit,*" she said and then disappeared in a shimmer of light.

Charlotte stared at the spot where Elara had been and wondered if it had been a dream. But as she looked at the worried and confused faces of her parents, she knew it wasn't.

Her father was there and alive, and she threw herself at him, hugging him for all she was worth. "Oh, Dad."

His arms went around her, and then he knelt down so he could hold her more tightly. "Why do I have the feeling that I'm going to need to start taking heart medication when you explain to us what just happened?"

Charlotte laughed through her tears and pulled back. "What did she say before she left?"

He brushed a stray lock of hair from her face, his long fingers gently caressing her cheek, and a curious smile came to his lips. "She said, 'Happy Christmas.'"

SIMON RAN A HAND through his hair as he paced back and forth across the kitchen. He paused and put a hand to his forehead, the beginning of a headache already starting.

"Let me see if I have this straight," he said, knowing he did, but needing to repeat it aloud until the reality of what his daughter had just done settled in.

From her perch on a stool at the counter Charlotte sighed, pulling the blanket around her shoulders. She'd changed out of her cold, wet clothes, but the cold still clearly clung to her.

Simon fixed her with a glare, but there wasn't much in it. He was too tired, too frightened, too humbled to be angry.

"You discovered that there was a curse on the family," he said.

"Yes," Charlotte said and gave him a quick nod of confirmation.

"And you tried to tell us but we . . . were unable to keep the thoughts in our heads."

Charlotte nodded again. "It was so frustrating!"

Elizabeth squeezed her shoulder. "More hot chocolate?"

Charlotte held up her mug with a smile. Elizabeth took it and poured her another from the pan on the stove.

Simon pushed out a breath. Elizabeth was taking this much better than he was. It was, frankly, rather annoying.

"And so you took it upon yourself," he continued, "to break the curse."

"I had help," Charlotte reminded him.

"Yes. The ghosts of my ancestors. Perfectly normal."

Elizabeth gave a laugh. "Well, normal for us."

He sighed again, slowly winding his way back to the part of the story that was going to give him a lifetime supply of nightmares. "And once you discovered what you had to do, give three gifts, you ran out in the middle of the night—"

"I had to," Charlotte protested. "You would've—I had to."

Simon regarded her as she stared down into her mug of hot chocolate.

He was angry, to be sure, but it was unfair to take it out on Charlotte.

He pinched the bridge of his nose. "Yes." She'd explained about the ticking clock; the idea that he would perish at sunrise must have been terrifying for her.

He sat on a stool next to hers, reached out, and put his hand on her arm. She flinched slightly but tried to pretend she hadn't.

"You're hurt," he said.

She pushed up her sleeve to show him a small bruise on her forearm.

"It's okay. I hit my arm when I fell in the well."

Simon's heart clenched at that—fell in the well—although, in truth, it hadn't unclenched since they'd discovered she was missing. "And that was before you offered your life to the witch of the Dark Woods."

Charlotte winced. "It sounds bad when you put it like that."

"Charlotte . . ." He was at a loss for words. "You must promise me you will never do something like that again. The thought of you . . ."

This time she reached out to him, her small hand gripping his.

"You must promise me," he said. He could scarcely fathom the emotions her near-sacrifice evoked in him and tried to put them away to consider privately later. "It is my job to protect you. Not the other way around."

"We protect each other," she said, sounding so much like her mother it made him both fiercely proud and terribly afraid at the same time.

"You're a child. Our child," Elizabeth said, putting her arm around their daughter's shoulders. "Let us do the protecting for now."

Charlotte nodded and then hastily added, "Unless there's another curse and—"

"There are no more curses," Simon vowed, silently praying he was right. There had better not be. "I simply forbid it." He could not go through this again.

"Do you think the others are already gone?" Charlotte asked. "Phineas and Ambrose and Nicky?"

"I don't know, darling," he said, "but wherever they are, I'm sure they're very grateful."

She nodded and looked a little dejectedly into her mug. "I think you would have liked them—well, Phineas . . . eventually." Her voice trailed off into silence. Simon and Elizabeth shared a pained look.

"We have a surprise for you," Elizabeth said. "Nothing as grand as breaking a four-hundred-year-old curse, mind you, but it's not bad."

Charlotte brightened a little. "What?"

DESPITE IT BEING LAST minute, literally, Elizabeth deemed the Grey Hall Christmas and Yule party a rousing success. The Carters and Fiona Prince had worked tirelessly to help her, preparing food and drink for the impromptu gathering that afternoon.

The turnout was even better than she'd dared hope. It seemed a lot of people from the village were willing to give up a few precious hours of their Christmas to get a glimpse inside Grey Hall. That in and of itself was reason enough for the choice she and Simon had made.

Three or four dozen people milled around the great hall, nibbling on the hastily-thrown together appetizers courtesy of Fiona and drinking more of that amazing wassail. The music of Tchaikovsky, Corelli, and Mozart floated through the hall, drifting from "The Nutcracker" to "Ave Maria." There was even a selection of more modern music including some that a Spotify user, The Pagan Granny, claimed were Yule appropriate.

The lights from the elegant Christmas trees twinkled in the candlelight. Charlotte had even dragged their little Charlie Brown tree out into the main room, putting it on a table in the center of the hall.

This was how Elizabeth had always envisioned Grey Hall at Christmas—bright and bustling with life and good cheer.

She was busy talking with Fiona when Simon signaled to Charlotte to turn off the music. He climbed up a few stairs of the grand staircase and cleared his throat. "If I might have your attention, please."

Slowly, the crowd quieted.

"I realize that for many of you this is your first time at Grey Hall, and while I am glad you are here today, I am ashamed that this is the case. The village of Greyswood has always supported Grey Hall, and we have not returned the kindness."

A curious murmur rose from the crowd.

"We have kept ourselves separate, above, some would say, but that ends here today. We are a part of Greyswood. I grew up in this village, and it took me . . ." he frowned, shaking his head, "far too many years to realize what it means to me. It is our home. Our collective home and past."

He glanced over at Elizabeth. "It is much too easy to run from such things. To put them behind us, forget those that which give us pain. However, sometimes we must embrace the past in order to explore our future."

The crowd chittered quietly, although everyone looked a little confused.

"Get to the point," Elizabeth whispered.

Simon chuckled. "As my wife says. I know many of you have heard the rumors that we are going to sell Grey Hall. I want to put that to rest here and now. We are not."

This was met with a surge of approval.

"We do, however, plan to be better neighbors. Greyswood is struggling, like so many villages and towns across England. But this is our village, and we're not letting go of it so easily. I've met with some of the village council," he went on, searching out Mr. Kingsley and Mr. Booth, "and made a promise to them that I will repeat to you here now. We—my wife, my daughter, and I, the Cross family, will do whatever it takes to renew Greyswood, to fund the restoration of our heritage—the old church, the folly, and the holy well."

His eyes flicked to Charlotte, who beamed with pride.

"We owe it to our future to not forget our past," he went on. "And we must always remember that hhere is more that joins us than divides us. And now, during Christmas and Yule, this season of giving, we must focus on what truly matters—each other."

Someone in the crowd called out, "Happy Christmas!" and cheers went up all around.

"Happy Christmas and Blessed Yule," Simon said, catching Fiona's eyes.

CHARLOTTE ENJOYED THE PARTY, but she couldn't help but feel something was missing. When the guests started to leave, she slipped out of the room and made her way to the library, but before she got there both of her parents caught up to her. They'd been keeping a close eye on her all day, not that she could blame them.

"Charlotte?" her father asked, a not-so-subtle warning in his voice. "Where are you off to now?"

She sighed and looked up at them both. "I'm not going to run off into the forest again. I told you."

"Yes, you told us," her mother replied as if she hadn't just promised again.

"I was going to the library to see if . . . well, to see if they were truly gone."

Simon's expression softened. "I would think once the curse was lifted . . ."

"I know," Charlotte said, unable to keep the sadness from her voice. She really wanted to see them one last time. She couldn't have done any of this without them. "But maybe?"

Her father chuckled and put a hand on her shoulder, steering her toward the library. "Maybe. And if so, I'd like a chance to meet them myself."

"You would?"

"They are . . ." he nearly laughed when he said the last word, but she could tell that he meant it, "family, after all."

"And I do love a good ghost," Elizabeth added.

Charlotte's hopes lifted when her father opened the library door, but it was empty.

"Hello?" she called out.

"Maybe they had no choice but to leave when the curse was broken?" her father suggested. "There isn't much documented about curses of this sort and the spirit world. In Japan, there are supernatural beings known as Yūrei that—"

"Not now," Elizabeth said softly, putting a stilling hand on Simon's arm.

Charlotte was crestfallen. She really thought she'd have the chance to see them again.

"I'm sure they'd say goodbye if they could," Elizabeth said.

"And so we shall!" Phineas announced as he strode through the bookcase, Ambrose and Nicky close behind. "Forgive us, my dear, we have been . . . elsewhere."

Charlotte bounded forward.

"Well, that's an entrance," Elizabeth mused.

"I'm so glad," Charlotte said. "I thought you'd left."

"We do not have much time, I am afraid," Phineas said and then looked away from her to study Simon and Elizabeth. "You should be proud of your Charlotte. She is exceptional."

"We are," Simon assured him. "You must be Phineas."

He gave them a bow.

"And you're Ambrose and Nicholas," Elizabeth said, coming closer.

"And *you* are lovely," Nicky said with a very appreciative smile.

Simon frowned at that, stepping closer to his wife. "And married."

Elizabeth laughed. "You can't be jealous of a ghost."

"Were I not one he would have ample reason," Nicky said meaningfully.

Phineas sighed. "Imagine living with that for a hundred years."

It had been less than a week, but so much had happened. Charlotte hated the idea that she might never see them again.

"I don't want you to go," she admitted. "I know it's selfish, but . . ."

"I don't want to go either," Ambrose whispered, leaning down to be closer to her height. "I've not had so much fun in centuries."

"I don't suppose . . ." Charlotte ventured.

"I am afraid not, child," Phineas said. "We are called elsewhere."

She nodded, trying to be brave about it. "Will I ever see you again?"

Phineas seemed to think about that, his eyes narrowing so much like her father's when he was deep in thought. "I do not know," he admitted finally. "There is always a possibility, but you have your whole life ahead of you, and I have . . . whatever awaits me on the other side."

"I'll miss you. All of you."

"And we you, child," he said gently and then straightened, clearing his throat and glancing at the others. "It is time."

"I . . ." Charlotte began, then shook her head, settling on the only thing left to say. "Happy Christmas."

He chuckled, a deep resonant sound. "Yes. I feel for once it actually is."

He gave her a small bow, and Ambrose and Nicky waved goodbye as they faded away. For the first time in a very, very long time it was indeed a happy Christmas at Grey Hall.

THE END

Don't miss the next adventure, sign-up for Monique's new release newsletter here.

If you enjoyed this book, please consider posting a short review.

Other Books by Monique Martin

Out of Time Series

Out of Time: A Time Travel Mystery (Book #1)
When the Walls Fell (Book #2)
Fragments (Book #3)
The Devil's Due (Book #4)
Thursday's Child (Book #5)
Sands of Time (Book #6)
A Rip in Time (Book #7)
A Time of Shadows (Book #8)
Voyage in Time (Book #9)
Revolution in Time (Book #10)
Expedition in Time (Book #11)
Race Through Time (Book #12)
That Time in Paris (Book #13)
Secrets in Time (Book 14)

Out of Time Christmas Novellas

In Time for Christmas
Christmas in New York
The Christmas Express
Christmas in London
The Christmas Curse

Saving Time Series

Jacks Are Wild (Book #1)
Aloha, Jack (Book #2)
Nairobi Jack (Book #3)
Maverick Jack (Book #4)

The Blaze Series

The Blaze (Book #1)
Mirror (Book #2)
Legacy (Book #3)

Hollywood Heroes Series

The Frame (Book #1)
The Curse (Book #2) - coming soon!

ABOUT THE AUTHOR

Monique was born in Houston, Texas, but her family soon moved to Southern California. She grew up on both coasts, living in Connecticut and California. She currently resides in Southern California with her naughty Siamese cat, Monkey.

She's currently working on an adaptation of one of her screenplays, several short stories and novels, and the next book in the world of *Out of Time*.

moniquemartin.weebly.com
or email
writtenbymonique@gmail.com